THE RACE

GOLDEN FILLY SERIES

THE  RACE

LAURAINE SNELLING

BETHANY HOUSE PUBLISHERS
MINNEAPOLIS, MINNESOTA 55438

Published by Bethany House Publishers
A Ministry of Bethany Fellowship, Inc.
6820 Auto Club Road, Minneapolis, Minnesota 55438

Printed in the United States of America

Library of Congress Cataloging-in-Publication Data
Snelling, Lauraine.
   The race / Lauraine Snelling.
      p. cm. — (The Golden filly series ; bk. 1)
   Summary: Tricia learns to trust in God as she deals with the
problems of her father's serious illness and her mother's disaproval
of Tricia's involvement with horse racing.

   [1. Horse racing—Fiction. 2. Family problems—Fiction.
3. Christian life—Fiction.] I. Title. II. Series: Snelling, Lauraine.
Golden filly series ; bk. 1.
PZ7.S677Rac 1991
[Fic.]—dc20   90–23609
ISBN 1–55661–161–7   CIP
                                         AC

The Race is dedicated to my daughter Marie
who won her race and now wears her crown.

LAURAINE SNELLING is a full-time writer who has authored several published books, sold articles for a wide range of magazines, and written weekly features in local newspapers. She also teaches writing courses and trains people in speaking skills. She and her husband Wayne have two grown children and make their home in California.

Her life-long love of horses began at age five with a pony named Polly and continued with Silver, Kit, Rowdy, and her daughter's horse Cimeron, who starred in her first children's book *Tragedy on the Toutle*.

CHAPTER 1

The rising sun peeked through feathery mist.

Two thoroughbreds rounded the far turn on the three-quarter mile track at Runnin' On Farm. Side by side, both riders stood high in their stirrups to hold the surging animals under control.

"Now, Tricia!" Hal Evanston, the rider on the gray, shouted above the thunder of pounding hooves.

His daughter, Tricia, nodded, loosened the reins and crouched back in the saddle, her face almost buried in two-year-old Spitfire's black mane. "Okay, boy," she whispered to the colt's twitching ears. "Let's see what you can do."

The colt leaped forward. He snorted, then settled into ever-lengthening strides. The white fence blurred as Spitfire gained speed. Beside him, old gray Dan'l valiantly attempted to keep pace. Another furlong and the black was stretched out, running free. The gray dropped back, blowing hard.

Tricia urged the colt on, using her hands and feet. She thought about the whip in her hand but decided against it.

"Come on, baby," she crooned. "Let it out. Let's go all the way." The horse gave a little more. His heavy breathing drowned out the thunder of his hooves. As they passed the entrance gate, Tricia remembered her father's instructions. She eased back on the reins.

"That's enough for now, fella." She chuckled as Spitfire shook his head. She pulled the reins tighter, rising in the stirrups to gain more control. Gobs of lather splashed past her as he shook his head again. Tricia ducked her face into his sweaty mane for protection.

"Come on, Spitfire," she coaxed him. "You gotta slow down. We're in cool-down time now. You'll get to race again. I promise."

The feisty colt slowed to a canter, tossing his head and playfully fighting the snafflebit. The desire to race on around the track screamed from every taut muscle. His blue-black coat was lather-flecked and dripping wet but he'd finally tasted real racing. Centuries of selective breeding had led to this event. He was a thoroughbred in every line and hair of his seventeen-hand, long-legged body.

Tricia settled back in her short-stirruped racing saddle as the horse slowed to a trot, then a walk. *Man, oh man*, she thought, *Dan'l's never been this fast. Maybe, no, not maybe. For sure this horse is going to do it for us.* She pushed her goggles up on her head and dreamed ahead. *Only one month to go before the season opens. Twenty-eight days until my birthday. Then I'll be sixteen and old enough to ride at the Portland Meadows Race Track. To win! I know we can do it. Spitfire and me.*

She stroked the animal's arched neck. "We'll do it, won't we, fella?"

Spitfire danced faster when he felt the reins loosen. His ears pricked forward as he recognized the gray walking ahead of them. The black blew. He tossed his head. He tried to take the bit in his teeth but Trish foiled his attempt when she tightened the reins.

"Thought you'd try something, didn't you?" She gentled him with her voice. As they came up on Dan'l, Spitfire jogged sideways. His front legs crossed one another, like a dancer in a *pas a deux*.

"Well? What'd you think? Wasn't he fantastic? Oh, Dad, I've never ridden so fast in my whole life. He'll do it for us, won't he?"

"Wait a minute." Hal laughed as he held up a gloved hand. "Give me a chance to answer. Which question is most important?"

Trish chuckled. "He was *so* good!"

"Better than just good." Hal nodded. "Makes me more sure than ever that Spitfire's the one we've been waiting for. I think he has the speed to win."

Trish grinned at her father, but her grin turned to a frown as she watched him bend over Dan'l's gray neck. He coughed until he gasped.

"You okay?" She reined the side-stepping black down.

Hal nodded. "Just too much dust." He wheezed as he spat the choking phlegm at the ground. "I'm fine now."

"You sure?"

"Of course I'm sure," he snapped. "Don't start cross-examining me, Babe."

Trying to hide her hurt feelings, Tricia jerked the reins. Spitfire reared in surprise, then crowhopped in place. "Sorry, fella," she muttered as she straightened him out into a slow trot again.

"Sorry I barked at you." Hal trotted the gray even with Tricia and her sweating mount.

"That's okay," Tricia shrugged. "But Dad—"

"No 'buts.' Let's talk about something else." Hal tapped her gloved hands with his whip. "How did Spitfire feel when you pulled him up? Did he have more to give?"

"I think so." Trish settled back in her saddle. "But he was tiring."

"That's just conditioning. Did he want to keep running?"

"Did he ever! With another horse pushing him, I think he'd really have gone."

"Well, poor old Dan'l just wasn't in shape to give that youngster a real run for his money." Hal patted his mount's sweaty neck. Dan'l twitched his ears, then tossed his head. As he side-stepped, pulling against the reins, Hal laughed. "I know, old man. You love to run, too."

Trish wanted to reach over and hug the old horse. He was her favorite; the horse who had helped her learn to be a jockey. She'd been exercising him for the last five years, getting ready for her first race at Portland Meadows Race Track.

"We're getting close, huh?" She smiled at her father.

Hal nodded, his understanding immediate. So often they read each other's minds, not needing to finish their comments.

"We've got a lot to do." Hal loosened his reins to bring Dan'l into a canter. "Not the least of which, you'll be late for school if we don't hustle."

"I guess so." Tricia leaned forward. "Come on, Spitfire. I'd rather ride some more but we had better mind the boss."

At the same moment she noticed the woman and young man leaning on the fence by the gate. A purebred sable collie sat obediently at their feet, never taking his eyes off the moving animals. He whined softly.

"Easy, Caesar." Marge Evanston, Tricia's mother, patted the dog's silky head.

Trish's twenty-year-old brother David stared at the stopwatch clenched in his hand.

"How fast was he?" Marge asked. "I could tell from the grin on Tricia's face that he was good."

"Well, it looks like he did four furlongs in 48 and 2 and that's with no one pushing him. Give him some more training and—"

"He'll be ready for The Meadows." Despair echoed in her voice.

"Yeah. I think so."

"Oh, David, I don't want Trish racing at the track. She's fine around here but at the track . . . it's too dangerous. A race track is no place for a young girl."

"Female chauvinist?" David teased.

"No, just trying to protect my daughter."

"Come on, Mom. You worry too much. She'll be all right. You know how tough and independent she is." He patted his mother's arm. "Besides, she's been riding all her life. Racing our thoroughbreds is her big dream."

"Big dream or no. I've seen some of those jockeys after they've been scraped off the track. Even the best riders get hurt, let alone an inexperienced novice. It's no—"

"David!" Trish interrupted as she trotted up to the gate. "Did you see us?"

David grinned and held up the stopwatch. "Fantastic!"

"What's the time?" Tricia leaned forward as he waved the shiny gold watch on its chain.

At the sight of the unfamiliar glinting object, Spitfire half-reared and whirled to get away. Caught off-balance, Tricia grabbed instinctively around the animal's neck and dug in with her knees. Like a slow-motion picture, she catapulted from the horse's back and thumped on to the loose dirt of the track. Even as she hit the ground, Trish clutched one rein in her hand to keep Spitfire from backing away.

"Oof!" She grunted at the force of the impact. "Oh no, you don't!" She rolled to her feet to control the plunging horse. "Come on, Spitfire. It's only me. You're okay."

Hal swung Dan'l around to block the colt from taking off. In that split-second Marge and Hal made eye contact. *I told you so*, rang silently through the air as Marge spun around and headed for the house.

"Tricia . . ." David began.

"I'm fine." She kept her eyes on her horse. "I've been dumped before. Besides, my pride's hurt worse than my rear—I think."

"Well, if your pride's as dirty as your rear, you're in real trouble."

"Thank you, big brother." Tricia held the now-quiet horse's bridle with one hand and dusted herself off with the other. "Hey, Mom. What'd you think?" She looked to the fence where Marge had been standing with David, then at David. "Where'd she go?"

Hal and David shrugged in unison.

Tricia shook her head. "Not a good time to take a flying lesson, huh?"

Hal shrugged again and stared toward the house, disappointment clear in the droop of his mouth and shoulders. "Come on, Tee. These guys are hungry and so am I."

"But, Dad, I didn't get hurt. And Spitfire didn't mean to dump me. It was that stupid watch that scared him."

"I know." Hal answered as he walked his mount beside Tricia. "But you know your mother's worried that you could really get hurt on the racetrack."

"Sure. And a meteor could fall out of the sky and pound me into the dirt."

Hal chuckled.

"Or the school bus could sprout wings and kidnap me . . ."

"Now, Tee."

"Or I might get ptomaine poisoning from my cereal." Trish delivered the last with all the dramatic flair of a seasoned actress.

Hal laughed again. "Well, falls have happened to better jocks than you, you know." He nudged Dan'l into a trot. "But don't worry, I'll call the emergency wagon for you after I wash these horses down and feed them. Think you can hang on till then?"

"I'll try." Trish touched the back of her leather glove to her forehead. The wink her father gave her was all the applause she needed. "David?" she asked as he fell into step beside her. "How am I ever gonna convince Mom that I'm a careful rider?"

"Sure you are." David reached behind her to pat Spitfire's neck. "You just proved it."

"D-a-v-i-d!" She dug into his ribs with her elbow. "That fall was no big deal."

"To our mother it was. You know what a worrier she is. She's always worried about Dad at the track, and now you add to it. Besides, in her mind, girls shouldn't be racing horses, especially not *her* girl."

"Yeah, I should take dancing lessons and wear a frilly tutu. Maybe I should smear makeup on an inch thick too, and chase every guy in sight."

"Knock it off, little sister." David draped an arm around her shoulders. "No one said growing up was easy." He glanced at his watch. "You better move it or you'll be late for school, and you know what happens—"

"Okay. Okay. Don't remind me. I've already been late once and school's been going less than a week." She trotted toward the stables, Spitfire dancing behind her. "David," she called after him as he turned to the house. "You can muck out the stalls. It'll be good for you. Someone once told me it builds muscles."

"Got enough already." David flexed an arm, then whistled for Caesar. Together, they loped up the rise.

Tricia led Spitfire into his stall and cross-tied him. As she reached to loosen the saddle girth, she heard her father start to cough in the adjoining box stall. She pulled the racing saddle from Spitfire's withers, paused, then called, "Dad?" As the coughing continued, she slung the saddle over the lower half of the stall door. In frustration, she jerked her goggles and helmet off her head, only to run trembling fingers through her thick ebony hair. *If I could just go to him*, she thought. *But what if he yells at me again?*

The rattle of her father's struggling breath filled the stalls. Spitfire tossed his head, eyes rolling white at the strange sound.

Tricia crammed her gloves into her pocket, and green eyes flashing, stepped into the sunshine. She swung Dan'l's stall door open. Her father leaned against the wall. His body sagged as he choked for breath.

"Dad . . ." Trish shook his arm. When he turned, she saw bright red bubbles frothing from the corner of her father's mouth.

"Don't worry, Tee." The words rasped in his throat. "I'll be all right."

No you won't, Tricia thought. *Blood means more than allergies or a smoker's cough, like you've always claimed.*

CHAPTER 2

Dan'l snorted. He shoved his nose into Tricia's back. When that didn't get her attention, he blew in her hair. Feeling a burning in her eyes, she absently rubbed his soft nose.

"Oh, Dan'l," she whispered. "What are we gonna do?"

Hal coughed again. After he spat the choking mucus out of his throat, he pulled a handkerchief from his back pocket and wiped his mouth. When he saw the blood stain, he stared at his daughter.

"Honest, Trish. There's never been blood before." He shook his head. "Guess I better see a doctor right away, spare time or no spare time."

"Guess so."

Hal wrapped both arms around Trish. As he hugged her close, he absently rubbed the early morning stubble on his chin against her forehead.

Tricia felt a little more secure. Her father had always made everything all right. When she was little, he fixed the broken rope on her swing. He kissed her and put her back up on the pony when she fell off. All her life she'd tagged after him and David as they farmed and slowly built a business training thoroughbreds for the race-track.

Most of those years Hal had trained horses for other

breeders. It was only since Trish had turned ten that he'd had horses of his own to race. They still had horses in the stalls that belonged to other owners, but Tricia liked to work their own animals best. Since Dan'l was getting too old to race, they had Spitfire and his half-sister Firefly for this season and some real promising young stock for next year.

With her head against her father's chest, Tricia could hear the air rattling through his lungs. He wheezed, then gently pushed her aside so he could cough again.

"Short and sweet this time," he tried to joke as he took a deep breath. "See Ma, no cough."

Tricia wanted to join in their old joke from her bike-riding days. "See Ma, no hands" had been her password. Now all she could see was her father's pale face with sweat beading on his upper lip. While the horrid red bubbles had been wiped away, a dried-brown smear marked where they'd been.

"Oh, no." Hal checked his watch. "It's seven o'clock. I'll get the tack off these boys and you feed them. Then you've gotta get to school."

"I'll be late anyway so why don't I stay home today. I can catch up on some stuff around here while you and Mom go to the doctor."

"David can do the chores. You're going to school."

"But Dad—"

"Tricia." Hal gripped her forearms with calloused hands. "I'm going to be fine. Your staying home won't change anything but your grades." Tricia stared into his eyes, seeking an answer to the fear that gnawed like a beaver at the back of her mind.

"Really."

He turned her and lovingly swatted her on the seat.

"Now get going. These horses are hungry."

Sunlight turned the straw to gold as she shuffled toward the open door. Dan'l snorted. Spitfire whickered. Soft nickers passed down the row of white stalls as the horses begged for their feed. Tricia turned and looked at her father one more time. His tuneless whistle accompanied his hands as he uncinched the saddle. Suddenly, the morning was the same as any other; the tell-tale dab on his cheek the only sign of trouble.

Sucking in a deep breath, then letting it all out, Tricia stepped into the sunshine. "Be right back, fella," she promised Spitfire as she picked up the buckets and headed for the feed room.

After loading half a bale of alfalfa and the filled grain buckets into the wheelbarrow, Tricia hurried from stall to stall. She measured each animal's allotted grain into their feed boxes and threw a wedge of hay in each manger. After checking to see that all the animals but Spitfire and Dan'l had water, she stepped into the tack room as Hal finished hanging up the saddles and bridles.

"Ready?" she asked.

"Yep, but I don't think we'll race this time."

Tricia nodded. "That's okay. I've beaten you the last three mornings."

"I gave you a head start."

"Sure. Sure."

"You don't believe me?"

"Nope." Trish shook her head.

"What do you think I am?" Her father bent at the waist and with his right hand on his hip, limped for several steps. "A rickety old man?"

"Yup," Tricia responded, trying not to laugh. "Just a

worn-out falling-apart ancient old man." The two paced each other up the rise toward the house.

"See if I give you the fastest horse tomorrow morning," he growled, laughter showing in his hazel eyes. "Lady, from now on, you work old Dan'l."

"Nope. The old horse suits the old man."

Arm in arm, they mounted the three concrete steps to the deck off the back of the house. Vertical cedar siding on the walls set off the blossom-covered fuchsias hanging from the beams. Below the baskets, tubs of ruby begonias raced for first place in the blooming contest.

Tricia paused to look for the hummingbirds that dined every day on the drooping pink, purple, and white blossoms.

"Hustle, Tee," Marge called. "You're late again."

"Dad." Tricia clutched her father's arm. "You'll go to the doctor today?"

"Umm-m-m. See . . . there's a hummingbird. On the other side of the pink basket."

"Don't play games with me." Tension tightened Tricia's jaw. "If you don't tell Mom, I will."

"Now, Trish."

"I will."

"Okay. Okay." He raised his hands in surrender.

"What are you two so serious about?" Marge met them at the sliding glass door. "In case you haven't noticed, my girl, you're late."

Trish glanced at her mother, then stared into her father's eyes. Silence. *Why doesn't he tell her?* Tricia thought. *I'm not going to back down; not this time. I know there's something really wrong.* Unbidden, a prayer surfaced in her mind. *Make him well, God. He's the best father a girl could ever have.*

Hal took a breath, like he was preparing for a deep

dive. He patted Trish on the shoulder, then put his arm around Marge and walked into the family room with her.

Trish slid onto the stool by the door.

"It's about this cough I've had." He drew out a chair. "Sit down, Honey."

"That bad?" Marge laughed up at him as she sat.

"Ummm-mm, I think so. Ah-h." He rubbed her shoulders. "This morning I coughed up a bit of blood. The pain was so bad I nearly fainted."

"But Hal, you've always said—"

"I know what I've been saying. But there has been pain. Not much but . . ." He walked to the window and stood looking out. "I think it's getting worse."

"Why haven't you—?"

"I don't know." He ran work-worn fingers through his hair. "I was so sure it would go away. I quit smoking. Thought that would do it."

"But it hasn't."

"No."

Trish felt each word beat against her. His flat "no" rattled in the room.

After a long moment, Marge asked, "What exactly happened down at the barn?"

Hal told her the entire story and ended with, ". . . and there was just enough blood on my handkerchief to scare the living daylights out of me."

"And me," Trish whispered from her perch by the door.

Marge slumped in her chair, one arm over the back.

In the corner, the fish tank bubbled on, as though nothing unusual had happened. As if Trish's world hadn't just had a major hole punched in it. She could hear David singing in the shower. Off key. As usual.

"Guess I'll go wash," she said.

"Yes," her mother acknowledged, not taking her eyes off her husband's back. "I'll call the doctor as soon as the office is open. We'll go right in."

"Don't I need an appointment?"

"I'm sure they'll want to see you right away—" Her mother's voice was cut off by Trish's rap on the bathroom door.

"You about done in there?" she raised her voice to be heard above the warbler.

"In a minute," David interrupted his favorite song to answer.

That means more like five, Trish thought as she leaned her head against the door. "Time for me to eat first?"

"Yeah. Probably."

"Well, take your time. I'm late already." The sarcasm in her voice finally penetrated to the songbird in the shower.

"Hey, what's with you?" David shut off the faucets. "You always eat first. Why should this morning be any different?"

"David." Trish heard the shower door slam. She knew she should head for the kitchen but couldn't force herself to listen to her parents again. Instead she tapped the door again. "David, Dad coughed up blood this morning."

"He what!" Her brother jerked the door open.

"There was blood on his handkerchief and the side of his mouth after a coughing attack. His face was all gray—and sweaty."

With one towel tucked in around his waist, David leaned against the door jamb. Without taking his eyes from Trish's, he reached for another towel and began drying his curly hair. "Does he know what's wrong?"

"No. They're talking about going to the doctor."

"He never goes to a doctor. He must be worried."

"Yeah. Just says he'll wait for the great Physician to do His job."

"He's always been right. So far."

"Yeah. So far. But . . ."

David draped the towel around his neck. "Hurry up, kid. I'll drive you to school as soon as you're ready. And Tee . . ." he added as she closed the door behind her. "We better start praying."

"I have been."

A quick shower later, Tricia grabbed beige pants and a matching striped T-shirt from her closet and threw them on the bed. A moment's rummage in the bottom of the closet proved that her shoes were missing—as usual. Still kneeling, she glared around her room. It was in its normal state of disaster. Piles of clothing were strewn on the floor and hid the chair. Finding the mirror would take an Act of Congress. So what if she never combed her hair again?

"Trish?" Her mother's voice broke through her concentration.

"Yeah. Yeah, I'm coming." She glared around the room one more time. "Have you seen my rope sandals?"

"They're in the living room, right where you left them," her mother answered. "You know, if you'd pick things up . . ."

"I know. I know," Trish muttered to herself as she slammed the bathroom door shut. "Don't start in on me right now. I don't have time."

Ten minutes later, dressed, and mascara applied to her long dark lashes, Trish brushed her hair back and tossed the brush on the counter. *No time to try anything different today.* But then, when did she have time? The racing schedule would make her life even more hectic. Good thing she had second-year Spanish first thing in the morning. It was an easy class. Her junior year. Well, big deal. Racing was more important.

Trish stopped long enough to slather peanut butter on a piece of whole wheat toast and pour a glass of milk to finish in the car.

"Here's a banana too," Marge said as David honked the horn.

Pushing the sliding door closed with her elbow, Tricia heard her father coughing again. It sounded as though he couldn't get his breath, then he gagged. Trish turned to see him collapse into a chair.

David's honking urged her to hurry.

Torn in both directions, Trish slammed the glass door open again. "Dad?"

"Come on, Trish," David hollered. "You'll be late for second period at this rate."

"Get going, Tee." Her father waved. Sweat beaded on his forehead. "I'll be all right."

Trish turned and ran down the steps. The little red bubbles around his mouth filled her mind.

CHAPTER 3

The morning dragged like a limping turtle.

All Trish could hear in her mind was her father's choking cough. His white face was all she could see when she closed her eyes.

"Hey, Trish, you all right?" Rhonda Seabolt asked on the way to lunch. Trish and Rhonda had been best friends since kindergarten.

"Yeah, I'm fine." Trish tried to smile.

"You sure don't look it."

"Thanks a lot."

"No. I mean . . . well—"

"Rhonda?"

"What?"

"What would you do if you saw your dad coughing up blood?"

Rhonda stared at Trish's sober face. Hurrying students jostled them as they stopped in the middle of the hall. "I don't know. Are you sure? About the blood, I mean."

Trish nodded. "We were out in the stable after this morning's workout. It happened again just as David and I left for school—"

"Hey, you two," a familiar baritone voice interrupted them. "You're blocking the hall."

23

Trish glanced up at Brad Williams, their tall, lanky cohort in innumerable escapades. He wrapped an arm around each of the girls and herded them over to the wall. "Now, if your conversation is so all-fired serious, at least you won't get run over."

"Thanks, friend." Trish tried to smile but the corners of her mouth felt stiff. She felt herself gathering to run. What she needed right now was to huddle in the big chair in the living room at home and wait for her parents to return. Maybe, just maybe, the problem wasn't too serious. Maybe some kind of medicine would make her dad well again. Maybe Jesus would make him well right away. She groaned to herself. She hadn't even thought to pray again. Some Christian.

"Trish?"

"Ummm-mm."

"What can I do to help?" Rhonda shifted her books so she had a free hand to grab Trish's.

"What's going on here?" Brad looked from one stricken face to the other. "Trish, you look like you lost your first race." He lifted her chin with a calloused finger.

Trish glanced from Rhonda to Brad, then stared at her typing book. The more she talked about it, the worse it seemed.

Taking the hint, Rhonda said. "It's her dad. He was coughing blood this morning."

Brad stared at the wall above Trish's head. He shook his head, took a shuddering breath and looked deep into her eyes, searching out the pain that lurked behind her self-control. "When did this start?" he whispered.

"Well," Trish tried to think back, "he's been coughing for a long time. Just kept referring to it as 'his smoker's hack.' You know how he is."

Brad nodded.

"Then this morning in the barn . . ." Trish stared at the hurrying mob of students with unseeing eyes. "They're at the doctor's now."

"Would you like me to take you home?"

"I don't know." She pushed her hair off her forehead. "I wanted to go home a minute ago, but here I have something to keep my mind sort of busy."

"Do you need help at the stables?"

"I don't think so. David's there."

"Well, if you need anything . . ."

"Sure, thanks." *What I need, you can't give,* she thought. *No one can.*

"Starving won't help." Brad took both girls' arms. "Let's go eat before the food's all gone."

Trish attempted a smile. She knew Brad was trying to make things easier for her. He'd been that kind of friend for years. Her mother often laughed about having four kids instead of two. David was the oldest, Brad next and finally the Siamese twins, Rhonda and Trish. All four had dreamed of being jockeys when they grew up but the boys had grown so big they made jockeys look like midgets. Rhonda had switched her concentration to showing gaited horses, so that left Trish to carry the farm silks to glory. Together they had voted on stable colors, crimson and gold. Hal teased them about being in a rut since those were their school colors, but they had stuck by their decision. Trish would wear crimson and gold all the way to the winner's circle.

Trish and Rhonda made their way to the salad bar. Like a robot, Trish greeted the serving attendant and filled her plate. Her shoulders slumped when she saw other students sitting at their table in the back of the room. There'd be no time for real talking, no privacy.

She felt like hiding. The walk across the room suddenly seemed too far, too difficult. Why, just this morning everything had been fine and now her favorite person in all the world was . . . she refused to finish the thought.

She juggled her purse and tray to free one hand. With it, she brushed back her wayward bangs. *We're winners,* she thought. *Dad always says "quitters never win and winners never quit."* She marched across the room.

"You want to sit somewhere else?" Rhonda asked from behind her.

"No. That's okay." Trish set her tray down. "Besides, everything else is full."

A chorus of "hi's" greeted the two as they pulled out their chairs. The familiar din of the lunchroom made talking below a shout difficult, so Trish concentrated on her salad.

"Still watching your weight?" Doug Ramstead, quarterback on the varsity football squad, pulled his chair close so he could shout in her ear.

Trish nodded. "Good thing I love salads."

"How long till you race?" He leaned nearer and lowered his voice. A lazy lock of blond hair fell over his forehead.

"The season starts October first, but we won't be in the first races. Dad has us scheduled for the Meadow's Maiden. That's a race for untried colts."

"Bet you can't wait."

"We're not ready yet. Spitfire still has more conditioning."

"Ugh. Don't even use that word." Doug shoved back his tray and leaned on his elbows.

"Workout was rough, huh?"

"Worse. Thought I was gonna heave my guts out." He

rubbed his biceps. "And my arms . . . I've been haying most of the summer, then weight training since the beginning of August. Coach Sey, the new man, makes old Smith look like a kindergarten teacher."

"How's the team look?" Trish chewed on her straw.

"Pretty good. This just might be our year." He turned partway so he could look at her. "What about you? Doing any lifting? I haven't seen you in the weight room."

"Yeah. I've been using David's old set at home. I just can't fit in the time to work out here."

"Could you fit in the party after the game on Friday?" He spoke right in her ear.

Trish felt a tiny shiver as his breath tickled her earlobe. She drew back at the unfamiliar sensation. "Can I tell you later? I'm not sure what my dad has planned."

"Sure." His voice stayed close. "But Trish, I'd really like to take you."

"Thanks." Trish spun her straw in her milk carton. "I'd like to go with you."

Doug pushed his chair back and stood, at the same time dropping a hand to her shoulder. "See ya."

Trish watched as the broad-shouldered quarterback made his way across the room with his tray. *You'd think he'd be a snob with all the attention he gets*, she thought. But he wasn't. His smile was as real as the hay bales he'd hoisted. And he even said "hi" to the giggly freshman girls, most of whom pushed Trish's patience to the limit. Going out with Doug Ramstead would be fun. But. There was always that "but" during racing season. Morning workouts came too early for her to stay out late. But just this once . . .

Rhonda poked her in the ribs. "Did he really ask you out?"

"Listening in, huh?" Trish turned her attention back to the table.

"Not really." Rhonda shrugged, then leaned closer as Trish toyed with another bite of lettuce. "You going?"

"I don't know." Trish glanced up to find Brad staring at her from across the table. "It's still a week away."

"David and I thought the four of *us* would go together—like always," Brad said. "It'll be his last night home."

"Of course!" Trish thumped her fist on the table. "How could I forget?"

"All that hunk had to do was say 'Hi,' " Rhonda laughed, "and your—"

"And my brain went into orbit," Trish finished for her. "I know what you're thinking."

"Well," Brad rocked his chair back on two legs. "That's the way it looked to us, huh, Rhonda? You two were sitting pretty close—"

"Brad Williams, I—"

"Now don't get your Irish temper up, Tee. It's not good for your digestion." Brad ducked as Trish faked a pitch with her milk carton.

"Sometimes you two go too far." Trish picked up her tray and joined the line to leave it at the dish window.

"Do you want a ride home after school?" Brad asked as they headed back to their lockers. "Or do you have something going?"

"No. I mean, yes, I want a ride home. The bus takes too long. I've got to lunge some colts this afternoon and Dad's gonna shoe . . ." Trish abruptly stopped as she remembered the scene in the stall that morning. With her notebook clutched to her chest, she rubbed her arms as if to warm herself.

"You okay?" Rhonda touched her arm.

Trish turned from staring into the trophy case without seeing. "Ummm-mm." She nodded. "See you later." She turned the corner to her locker. *Only three classes to go. Maybe, just maybe,* she thought. *No, not maybe.* She could hear her dad telling her to be positive. She had his words memorized: *When you want something really bad, picture it in your mind as already happening.* He'd drilled it into her since she was tiny. *Picture it in your mind.*

Trish swung her locker door open and leaned into the island of shelter it created. She scrunched her eyes shut. The picture she forced onto the backs of her eyelids was familiar: Her father kneeling in front of a gray gelding, taping the forelegs. Whistling off-tune. Breathing easily.

Until the coughing attack.

God! Help! her mind screamed. She grabbed her chemistry book and dashed toward the classroom, unaware of the people she bounced against. *Make him better; make him better.* Her mind pounded the beat for her feet.

Trish gritted her teeth to keep the tears from falling. Better wasn't good enough. *Please, God, I don't want him to be sick. He's always said, "You can do anything." Please!*

She slid into her seat as the bell rang.

"Hand in your assignments," the teacher said. "And turn to page 51."

Trish forced her mind to the job at hand. Her groan joined the universal lament of students unprepared.

I forgot it was due today! her thoughts took over again. *I haven't even started it. Great. I'd planned to do it during second period and lunch hour. He'll never let me turn it in late, either.* She looked at page 51. Without the first assignment finished, this one could have been written in a foreign language. In fact, some of the symbols were.

Trish shook her head. And David thought chemistry was fun. She sank lower in her seat and tried to pay attention.

The next class was no easier. By the final bell she'd responded with a blank stare to the teacher's question, mumbled, "I don't know" because she couldn't think, and been accused of daydreaming.

The drive home wasn't much better. Even Rhonda didn't indulge in her usual chatter as Brad drove up the curving driveway at Runnin' On Farm. The pick-up was gone. David's car was missing too.

Maybe Mom's shopping. Tricia's mind clutched at any idea.

Caesar barked a welcome. Except for him, the place was deserted.

"Do you want us to stay?" Rhonda asked.

"No." Trish shook her head. "I've got too much to do."

"I'll be back over as soon as I change," Brad said, ignoring her comment. "I know you'll need some help if your dad's been gone all day. And besides, he may not feel much like working in the barn after being at the doctor's."

"I've got a dentist appointment," Rhonda said, "but I can come after that."

Trish nodded, grateful for caring friends. "I'll call you if I need you."

"No. I'll be right back. I haven't gotten to exercise horses since David's been home for the summer. He took my job away, remember?"

Trish waved as the blue Mustang pulled away, then leaned over to hug the regal collie. "Mom? Dad?" she called as she opened the front door.

The stillness of the empty house wailed "no one home."

CHAPTER 4

Trish dropped her books on the entry table and headed into the kitchen for food and messages. David's note, stuck on the fridge door with a strawberry magnet, read, "Trish, Mom called from the hospital. They admitted Dad and she needed someone with her."

Slowly Trish removed the note and read it again. It was pretty plain. "They admitted Dad," she said aloud. *Then*, her mind reasoned, *the doctors think it's serious too. 'Course, that way he can get better faster. But the hospital . . . only Grandma went there—and she died.* Absently, she chose an apple from the bowl on the table, opened the fridge door, took out the milk and poured herself a glass. She felt like a mechanical doll, doing routine things without thinking.

You said You could take care of everything, God. How about this? Can You really heal my dad, like he says You can? Please, if You could just make it be something simple . . . They've got medicine for everything now. Just let him get the right medicine and come home. I need him!

Eating her snack with little enjoyment, Trish made her way to her bedroom to change clothes. The mess was still as she'd left it. No good fairies came during the day to repair the damage.

Trish dropped the apple core in the wastebasket. On

31

a huge poster on her wall, three thoroughbreds raced for the finish line, reminding her of the animals and stalls that needed to be taken care of.

"Good thing Brad is coming," she muttered. "There's lots to be done." She glanced around at the piles of clothes, dirty and clean all jumbled together. The unmade bed invited her to take a nap, but instead she tossed her pants and shirt on one of the mounds and scrambled to find a clean pair of jeans. A car horn sounded as she pulled a cut-off sweatshirt over her head.

"Coming," she shouted out the open window, then dashed down the hall to find her boots. At least they were by the door where they belonged. The horn sounded again.

"Brad, you idiot, I'm coming," she muttered to herself. Once out the door, she trotted to where Brad lounged against the fender of his metallic-blue Mustang. "How'd you get here so fast?"

"Fast?" He held up his watch for her to see. "It's been forty-five minutes. What have you been doing? Daydreaming?"

"Uh—huh—I mean, no," Trish shook her head. "David went into Vancouver to be with Mom. They admitted Dad to the hospital."

"I'm sorry, Tee." Brad touched her shoulder. "You want me to drive you in there?"

"No! Not now." She stared off at the stables. "I mean, uh, someone has to do the chores around here. We can't all be running in to the hospital." Trish cleared her throat as she leaned down to stroke the insistent Caesar. "Besides, Dad needs me here. There's so much left to do before the season starts." She took a deep breath, silently promising herself to think about that later.

"Well, then let's get at it." Brad bowed. "Brad Williams, horse feeder, trainer, mucker-outer, at your service."

"The pay's not so good."

"Madam, I am c-h-e-a-p labor. What I do, I do for love." Way off key, Brad crooned one of the latest hit melodies.

"Yeah, love of Mom's cookies." Trish grinned at his antics.

"Speaking of which . . ."

"No way. You get paid after you work, not before."

"You heartless slave driver." Brad tried one more pleading look. "Oh well," he bent over to talk to Caesar. "See how she picks on me?" The dog licked Brad's nose, and he brushed it off with the back of his hand. "Well, let's get at it."

"He's crazy, isn't he, Caesar?" Trish shook her head. The three of them, two long-time friends and the dog, jogged down the slope to the stables. The three white buildings looked peaceful in the late afternoon sunshine.

A chorus of whinnies greeted Trish's whistle. All down the line, horses' heads turned to greet her from the stable doors. Spitfire, in the near stall, tossed his head and wickered again. Dan'l, not to be out done, banged the door with his front hoof.

"Some greeting." Brad laughed.

"You guys just want out, don't you?" Trish rubbed Spitfire's soft black nose. He pushed against her shoulder, then nibbled at her hair.

"Careful, Goofy, you bit me yesterday." Trish rubbed his ears and stroked down the muscled neck. In the next stall, Dan'l reached as far toward her as his stall door permitted. His nostrils quivered in a soundless nicker.

"You old sweetheart." Trish rubbed his nose and on up to his favorite spot, just under his forelock. Dan'l draped his head over her shoulder, content to be scratched.

"What do you need me to do first?" Brad joined her in stroking the old gray.

"Let's get them on the hot walker, then you can muck out the stalls. I've gotta work with the younger colts and check on the mares. Those other two haven't been worked yet, either." She waved toward the two horses they were training for a new breeder.

"Fine with me." Brad grabbed the handles of the deep red wheelbarrow and followed her to Spitfire's stall.

Trish released the bolt and led the high-stepping black toward the hot walker, a circular exerciser that the horses moved themselves. She snapped the dangling lead rope to his halter, and as she left, slapped him lightly on the rump. The black reared slightly in sheer exuberance, then danced obediently around the worn track.

The girl smiled at his antics. "You're really something," she chuckled, pride in her eyes. Dan'l whinnied sharply and struck the door again. "I'm coming. I'm coming. Hang in there a minute."

After Dan'l and a bay filly joined Spitfire on the creaking hot walker, Trish approached the last stall on the west arm of the stable. "Hey, knock it off." She scolded the bay colt. "You're gonna beat the door to death." The colt glared at her, wild-eyed. Slowly Trish unlatched the stall door. "Easy now. Sorry you're the last."

The colt snorted. Trish slipped inside the door, then waited by the wall for him to calm down. "Easy, boy, easy now," she crooned, her voice gentle like a song. "You're just wasting time. If you'd behave you'd be outside already."

With a toss of his head, the colt stepped forward for the lead rope to be snapped to his halter. Trish rubbed his ears, then swung the door open and led him out.

Just as they cleared the door, a small piece of white paper tumbled by on the breeze. With a high squeal, the colt reared and struck out with one foreleg. The force jerked Trish off her feet.

"Oh no you don't," she muttered as her boots hit the ground again. Her arms felt like they had grown two inches. This time, as he reared again, she let the rope travel through her fingers. When he started down again, she seized his halter and smacked him on the nose.

Surprised, the colt shook his head and kept his feet planted on the ground.

"You finished smarting off now?" Impatience laced her voice. "That paper was nothing and you know it."

The colt looked around as if surprised at his own actions.

"Bit of a rodeo, huh?" Brad asked as she snapped the bay's lead rope to the hot walker.

"I guess." Trish rubbed her shoulder. "He's a spooky one."

"You sure you want to work him today?"

"Have to." Trish chewed her lip. "We told Mr. Anderson we'd have his horse ready for the first race."

"But Trish—"

"He'll calm down as soon as he gets to move around some. He always does." She turned toward the pastures. "Come on, Caesar, race you to the mares."

A frown creased Brad's forehead as he hefted the handles of the manure- and straw-heaped wheelbarrow. "Speaking of spooky," he muttered. "Girl, sometimes you worry me. There's nothing wrong with a little wholesome fear."

Having put the incident from her mind, Trish loped across the emerald turf. Two colts raced to the end of their pasture. The three mares in the adjoining paddock ignored the young frolicking in favor of lazy dreaming under the maple tree.

After a quick inspection, Trish patted the sorrel mare's shoulder and started back toward the barns. One of the mares coughed.

At the second cough, Trish wheeled back and checked each animal, ears, eyes, and nose. The sorrel with three white socks coughed again, stretching her nose toward the ground.

"Now, what?" Trish stroked the animal's satiny neck. She listened carefully as the mare breathed in and out. "No wheeze, old girl. You just trying to get some extra attention?" Trish chewed her lip as she watched and listened to the animal another minute.

"Remind me to watch her, Caesar old buddy," she patted the dog trotting beside her. "That's what Dad would do." She paused at the gate to the yearling pasture. Two of the colts raced back along the fence line. They plowed to a stop before her, then extended their muzzles to sniff her proffered hand.

Trish laughed at their antics but her attention zeroed in on the gray filly dozing against the back corner.

"What is this?" she questioned herself. "Sleepy time. Cough time. It's supposed to be training time. And I don't have time for anything else." Briefly she checked the filly for wheezing. She sounded fine. No mucus in her nostrils. But her eyes were droopy.

"Lethargic is the word." Trish closed her eyes to better recall symptoms she'd read in the medical dictionary. Only influenza came to mind. "I'll keep a close eye on you two," she promised with an extra pat. "We can't afford any sick animals."

Like well-trained puppies, the two colts dogged her footsteps back to the gate. When Trish snapped a lead shank on the colt named Samba and led him out of the gate, the other tried to follow. Caesar drove him back with a sharp bark.

"Thanks, old buddy." She swung the gate closed. "I can always count on you." Samba shook his head, then tried dancing in a circle. Playfully he struck out with a snowy forefoot.

"Nope. I've had enough of that kind of behavior today." Trish snapped on the rope. "You settle down right now." The chestnut colt rolled his eyes in mock panic, then ambled along beside her to the stable.

After Trish cross-tied him in an empty stall, she headed for the tack room to get an old soft bridle with a snafflebit.

"Need some help?" Brad wiped the sweat off his forehead. He parked the wheelbarrow in the breezeway. "That's one job done."

"Thanks, Brad." Trish rubbed the worn bit. "You can be his distraction."

"Great. First I'm a barrow-pushing slave and now I'm a distraction. When do we get to the fun stuff?"

"Like?"

"Oh, like racing two horses around the track. Eating cookies. Drinking Coke. You know, the important things in life."

"Yeah, I know. Your resident tapeworm is acting up again."

"Yup. I've gotta feed Fred at regular intervals." Brad patted his flat stomach. "Poor Fred."

"You nut. Forget Fred. We've gotta put the bit in Samba's mouth now."

The colt didn't bat an eyelash as Trish showed him the bridle with the silvery bit. He sniffed the leather, then looked over at Brad. Trish held the bit carefully to keep it from jangling as she rubbed the chilly metal against the colt's nose. He blinked and tried to shove his muzzle against her chest. Before he knew what had happened, Trish inserted a finger in the space behind his teeth, pried open his mouth and slipped the bit in place. At the same time, Brad slid the headstall over the animal's ears.

The colt snorted. He rolled his eyes, then shook his head. The bit and bridle stayed in place. With a sigh, Samba lowered his head again and nuzzled Trish for the treats she always carried in her pockets.

"Boy." Trish let out the breath she'd been holding. "That was easy." She palmed a sugar cube. "Here, you earned that, fella."

"Good job, partner." She shook Brad's hand as they left the stall. "We did it. We'll come back later and take that off. Give him time to play with the bit for a while."

"Now for the cookies?" Brad gazed soulfully toward the house.

"Nope. Now for the racetrack. You take Anderson's filly and I'll take the rowdy Gatesby."

"Maybe you should skip him today." Brad suggested. "You've already had one round with the beast."

"Nah-h. He just needs the exercise. Besides, we were

supposed to work him into the starting gate today."

"So?"

"We'll need extra hands to do that. Let's just take him up to the gate." Trish studied the colt, now pacing placidly around the ring. "That will give him a chance to look it over."

"Okay, Boss Lady. Let's go."

Within minutes they had the two animals saddled and ready. The bay colt stood calmly until Brad boosted Trish into the flat racing saddle. Before she could finish gathering the reins, the bay exploded. He reared, then pounded both front feet into the shavings. As Brad grabbed for the bridle, the colt lunged away from him.

Trish clamped her legs and tangled her fists in the colt's mane. "Whoa!" she commanded as she tried to tighten both reins, remain in the saddle and get control of the plunging animal.

"You crazy idiot!" Brad muttered as he leaped again. "Calm down!" This time he clamped his fist around one of the reins where it clipped to the bit. He jerked savagely. With a last snort, the bay stood still, his eyes rolling white.

"Would you lead him to the track?" Trish whispered as she fought to stop the trembling in her hands.

"You're as crazy as he is," Brad growled. "Put him away for now."

"No." Trish was adamant. "He's got to learn he can't act like this. He can't develop bad habits."

"Trish!"

"No, I'm okay. Lead us out there, then come with the filly. We'll trot a couple of laps, gallop a few more and then take them to the gates. Maybe he'll get the idea when he sees how easily the filly handles the gates."

Brad glared up at her. "Come on, then, stubborn." He pulled on the bridle.

"You talking to me or the horse?"

"Take your pick," Brad said without turning as he left them on the dirt track, then added, "Trish, be careful."

Willingly, as though he'd never caused a ruckus in his life, the colt struck out in a smart walk.

After both horses had cantered the track several times, Trish pulled the colt back to a walk, waiting for Brad to catch up. "Let's go 'round once together at a good clip, then breeze 'em once. Okay?"

"Fine with me," Brad replied, his grumpiness gone with the feel of obedient horseflesh beneath him. "Do you want me to push her?"

"Yeah. Let's give this colt a run for his money." She slapped her mount lightly on the shoulder.

At the marker, Trish gave the bay his head. "Come on, fella. You wanted to run so bad, so here goes." With a lunge he lengthened his stride, then settled into the rhythm. His pace quickened steadily as he heard the filly coming up on the inside. Trish tightened the reins, allowing the filly to pull even at the shoulders, then the nose.

The bay tugged at the bit, begging for a looser rein. "Okay, boy. Let's see what you can do." Trish let him have his head.

Slowly the bay inched ahead of the filly. First by a nose, then a neck. As the filly dropped behind them, Trish tightened the reins, slowing the animal's driving pace. Within a few strides, both animals were back to a slow gallop.

"Pretty good, wouldn't you say?" Trish shouted, riding high in the saddle.

"Mighty fine."

They slowed both animals to a walk. "Let's go work the gates while this guy is too pooped to fight." As they reached the entrance into the center field of the oval track, Trish heard a car horn. "We'll do this another time." She trotted back toward the gate, Brad beside her. David came up to meet them.

"How's Dad?" Trish slid to the ground.

"They're still at the hospital." David's voice caught in his throat. "Trish, it's bad."

"How bad?" She couldn't speak above a whisper as she rubbed the bay's nose.

CHAPTER 5

It can't be bad, Trish thought as she stared at David with unseeing eyes. *I've been praying—praying for this mess to be healed right away. Or at least for there to be some medicine to take care of it. Dad says God can take care of anything. Now Dad's the one that's sick. None of this makes any sense.* She shook her head. Her fingers automatically smoothed the horse's silky hide as she leaned against the colt's shoulder.

"Trish?" David spoke softly at first.

"Um-m-m."

"Listen to me." This time he shook her arm.

"I'm listening." Trish glared at him. "You're not saying anything."

"You were a zillion miles away."

"Well, I'm here now so tell me what you've found out."

"Here, Trish," Brad interrupted. "Let me take your horse with mine and get them cooled out."

"No. I'll come." She led the colt toward the stables. "Come on, David. We can walk and talk at the same time."

"Dad has cancer."

"Cancer!"

42

"In his lungs. That's why he's been coughing all this time."

"But people *die* from cancer!" Trish grabbed her brother's arm. "David, you're crazy. That can't be. I prayed—"

"Trish." David interrupted her frantic words. "Let me finish."

"No, David! Dad's not going to die. We've got too much to do here. The horses to train; the season's about to open. This is our year to win. No! He can't have cancer. No! No way!"

As Trish's voice raised to a shout, the colt's ears flattened. The whites of his eyes flashed.

"Trish!"

"No!" Unaware of anything but the pain crushing her heart, Trish jerked the reins.

Slashing black forelegs parted the air as the angry colt blasted his resentment at her thoughtless treatment. He reared, pounded the ground with furious hooves and reared again.

When he came down the second time, David leaped to seize the bridle. Trish tightened her hold on the one rein, the other flapped in the fracas. Together they brought the quivering colt to a standstill. As one they calmed him, their words running soothingly together.

"I'm sorry, fella," Trish mumbled as she stroked the flaring nostrils. "I forgot all about you. I know you can't understand, but things are really bad for us right now. Easy, I won't ignore you again."

Gatsby stamped one foreleg and blew—hard.

"You're okay now." David stroked the steaming neck on the off side.

"Boy, that was close." Brad dismounted to walk with them.

Keeping a wary eye on the horse, Trish asked, "David, are you sure the doctors said it was cancer?"

"Yeah," David bent his head. "I'm sure." Silently they each contemplated the horror until David blew his nose. "They're doing a biopsy tomorrow, but the X rays show a growth in both lungs. I saw them." He stopped the horse to face Trish. His red-rimmed eyes pleaded for her understanding to be quick. "They're huge. They said it's a miracle he's kept on so long."

"But when Aunty Bee had cancer, they just operated and took it all out."

"I know. I . . . well, you go talk to them tonight. Dad is expecting you. We'll go in as soon as the chores are done."

Trish shook her head. "I can't," she whispered.

"What did you say?"

Trish and the colt walked faster.

"Trish!"

"No, David. I just don't have time. I have a pile of homework, entry forms have to be filled out. I have to . . ." As they reached the barn, Trish snapped the two-way ties on to the colt's bridle. She filled a bucket with warm water and reached for the sponge and scraper. She wiped a hand across her eyes to clear the blurring. "I can't," she whispered. "I just can't."

David shook his head. "Don't be stupid, Tee. Of course you can." He picked up a scraper and the two guys copied her actions as they worked with the filly. Steam rose in a fluffy cloud when they rinsed the sweat off both horses. Off to the side, Caesar watched patiently, his dark brown eyes tracking Tricia as she swiftly groomed the colt.

On the hot walker, Spitfire nickered for attention.

Trish didn't see or hear any of it. *Think about it later,*

one side of her brain cautioned.

Now, God! Heal my dad, now! The other side screamed back. Her hands slowed as the war in her mind raged on. *I should have made him go to a doctor when his cough first started . . . why didn't Mom do something . . . why . . . oh, God . . . WHY?*

"Trish?" David touched her shoulder.

"What!"

"Brad and I'll feed, you go get the horses off the walker."

"Okay."

By the time the feeding was finished and the two Anderson horses were clipped to the hot walker, Trish had calmed the battle in her head. Instead of screaming, she felt numb, like a jaw full of novocaine.

"Does Dad have a phone in his room?" she asked as the three of them walked up to the house.

"Sure, but you can talk to him when we . . ."

Trish ignored him. "I've got to ask him about a mare that's coughing, and the gray filly is droopy."

"Trish, we'll—"

"No, David. You don't understand." She turned as they reached the steps. Pain clouded her green eyes. "I can't go there . . . to that—that place. At least not tonight." She shook her head. "Not now."

"But . . . but, Mom said . . ." David stuttered in his disbelief. "Trish, Dad needs you."

"I'll talk to him on the phone." The sound of the opening door punctuated her sentence. "Brad, you coming in for cookies and a Coke?"

Brad glanced at his watch. "No, think I'll pass for tonight. You gonna need help in the morning?"

"What do you think, David?" Trish stroked Caesar's

golden muzzle. The dog whined, low in his throat, always sensitive to her moods. Then he glued his haunches to her leg.

"We'll try to handle it tomorrow. If we can't get all the chores done, we'll call you. Okay?"

"Okay. But you know I'm available for whatever you need. Besides, I haven't gotten to do much riding for a long time. I'm sure Rhonda will pitch in too."

"Somehow . . ." Trish pledged, "somehow we'll get those horses ready. This is our year to win."

"Catch you later." Brad trotted off to his parked car, then turned. "Hey, David. When do you leave for school?"

Trish and David stared at each other.

"Oh my gosh," he muttered. "I'd forgotten all about that."

"Next weekend," Trish whispered. "You're supposed to leave next Sunday."

"What'd you say?" Brad leaned across the shiny roof of his car.

"It *was* next weekend," David called back. "But now? Who knows?"

Groaning, Trish threw herself down on the padded lounge chair. Caesar laid his head on her knee, brown eyes pleading for her to cheer up.

"What are we gonna do, old man?" she whispered, scratching his ears. "We just can't make it all alone. There's so much to be done around here." Her jaw tightened. "Well, we can if we have to. That's what Dad always says. God gives you the time and energy to do what you have to do. Right, David?"

Trish looked up from the dog to see her brother's stocky form propped against the house, his gaze staring across the pastures.

"Yeah, I guess so," he replied absently. David blew his nose again, dug in his pocket, pulled out a nail clipper and began clipping his nails.

Trish knew nail-clipping was David's way of buying time. Often she teased him about having the best manicure in Clark county. Today was not the time to mention that. Trish leaned over and rested her cheek on Caesar's warm head. His tongue flicked the tip of her nose. Before she got a full face cleaning, Trish turned away. Caesar thumped his feathery tail and dug his muzzle under her chin.

"Good old dog." She gently pulled his ears. "Always gotta get the last lick in."

Caesar put both front paws on her knees. As he stood looking her right in the eye, Trish laughed. "Get down, you big horse. What do you think you are, a lap dog?" The collie dropped to the deck, his nose and forepaws down, haunches and waving tail in the air.

"Can't play now." With one leap she reached the door. "Gotta get the phone." Caesar stopped patiently at the door. "It's for you," she called back to David.

Trish ignored her brother on the phone as she opened a large can of chicken noodle soup, poured it into two bowls, added water and popped them into the microwave.

"What was that all about?" she asked as she punched the timer.

"Getting rides back to Pullman."

"Sounded like a girl to me. I thought your rider's name was Danny."

"Yeah, short for Danielle. She's nice—blond hair, an education major. I've gone out with her a couple times. Anything else, nosy?"

"Yup. How come you haven't invited her out here to meet us?" Trish leaned against the kitchen counter.

David shook his head. "She's just a friend, for Pete's sake."

"Oh sure, just a friend," Trish mimicked his tone. The timer rang. "Ah, saved by the bell. Get the bread out while you're standing there. And the peanut butter." After setting the steaming bowls on the table, Trish returned to the fridge for milk and the raspberry jam. "Want anything else?"

"No, this is enough." David hooked the chair out with one foot.

Trish blew on her soup as she spread peanut butter and jam on her whole wheat bread. "So, what did you tell her?"

"Who?"

"The awesome blond, Danielle." She licked a drip of jam off her finger.

"Knock it off! I said I'd get back to her, but she better look around for another ride, just in case." David slurped a spoonful of soup.

"Just in case what?" Trish stopped chewing and stared directly at David.

"In case I don't go back."

"But David . . ."

"I mean for right now. You need me here. Mom needs someone with her. And how can I leave Dad? I can make it up later, no big deal."

"But what about your scholarship?"

"They'll have to hold it for later, I guess. Trish, none of that is important now." David shrugged. "It'll all work out, somehow."

"Mom's gonna be mad. Your college comes first with her."

"Not now it won't. All she needs to think about is Dad." David took a deep breath. "Besides, what else can we do?"

Trish went back to eating her soup. "I'm just glad it's not me telling her."

"Not to change the subject or anything, but hustle. We've gotta get to the hospital."

Trish choked on the mouthful of soup. "But I told you, I'm not going."

"Trish!"

"No! I'll call Dad as soon as I finish the horses." She shoved her chair back from the table. Stuffing the last of her sandwich in her mouth, she ran out the door, ignoring David's demands. Caesar bounded across the lawn after her.

Dusk was deepening into dark by the time Trish had returned all the horses to their stalls, wiped down and put away the tack and headed out to check on the coughing mare. She seemed well enough, so her next stop was the young stock pasture.

"Come on, Caesar," she called as he sniffed around a Scotch broom bush. "Leave the rabbits alone and let's find the filly."

As she climbed the board fence into the yearling's pasture, the two colts raced up and skidded to a stop. Both tossed their heads and nosed her for a treat.

"No treats." Trish pushed them away. "You haven't done anything to earn one." Both horses turned and followed her across the field, her flashlight playing out in front, searching for the missing animal.

Tricia crisscrossed the pasture from one end to the other. She checked the fences in case boards were down. The filly lay in the farthest corner. If it hadn't been for

Caesar, Trish might have overlooked the animal. Her shivering body blended into the shadows of the slight hollow.

Trish dropped to one knee beside the animal's head. "Oh, no," she whispered.

The gray head bobbed with a wrenching cough. Another shiver spasm rippled down the heaving sides. Trish searched her pockets. Not even a lead rope. Nothing.

CHAPTER 6

With a groan, Trish leaped to her feet. Her mind raced as fast as her pumping legs. *First, get the filly up and walk her to the barn. No. First get a lead rope. Do we have an empty stall away from the other animals? Yeah, I'll fork some straw in after I get her there. Then take her temperature and call the vet. Oh, if only Dad were here. I don't want to make these decisions. What if the filly dies? Oh, God, no—no! I won't think of dying. Please God, You said You'd help . . . all the time. Why are You so far away when I need You?*

When she reached the stable, Trish flipped on the light. Nickers and rustlings in the stalls told her she had surprised the sleeping animals. The thud of hooves on a wall warned her that Spitfire didn't take kindly to the interruption.

"Easy, fella," she called as she grabbed a lead rope off the nail and dashed back to the pasture. Caesar raced beside her.

"Dear God," she pleaded between harsh breaths. "Help me get her up and into the stall."

The filly still lay shivering in the hollow. When Trish petted the gray neck, her hand came away wet.

"Dew or sweat," she muttered. "I'm not sure. My feet

51

are soaked enough to make me think it could be dew. Let's hope so."

All the while her soft murmurings seemed to calm the shivering horse. With the lead rope snapped in place, Trish stood and leaned against it. The gray shook her head but made no effort to regain her feet.

"God, please." Trish wiped a hand across her forehead and wrapped the lead rope around her fist. "Come on, girl." The command rang across the hollow. "Get up!" Once more she leaned against the rope, her heels digging into the wet turf.

Caesar barked. The command sharpened when he nipped the filly on the rump.

The horse scrambled to her feet.

Trish scrambled to keep from landing on her seat.

"Wow!" She shook her head. "God, when You answer a prayer, You don't fool around."

"Thanks, Caesar." At his name the dog left his self-assigned position at the animal's hocks and nuzzled his slim nose into Trish's hand. "Good boy," she whispered. "Good job. Now let's get her up to the barn."

Slowly the three made their way to the lighted stables. Every time the filly stalled, a sharp bark from Caesar reminded her of the nip on the haunches. Trish led the droopy animal into the stall farthest away from the stabled horses, one kept for sick animals but rarely used. She clipped the lead rope into one of the barn rings, then snapped the cross-tie in place.

"I know you want to lay down," she stroked the sick animal. "But that will have to come later."

When she unlatched the door to the tack room, Spitfire nickered for attention. "Later, fella," she said as she reached inside the medicine cabinet for the thermometer and petroleum jelly.

The filly was too miserable to even flinch as Trish lifted the horse's tail and inserted the rectal thermometer. Her gray head drooped as far as the lead ropes permitted. The two minutes back-pedaled into what seemed like an hour while Trish's mind flipped pages in the medical dictionary searching for possible diseases.

"Whew! 104," she read after wiping the glass tube on her pant leg. "No wonder you're shivering, old girl. You've got a fever. Let's see what else." Swiftly she checked the animal for other symptoms. Droopy eyes, sweaty—can't hear any strange breathing; mentally she checked them off.

"Be right back," she patted the steamy neck. "Come on, Caesar. Let's call the vet."

The phone was ringing as Trish slid open the back door. "Runnin' On Farm," she could barely get the words past her gasps for air after the run to the house. "Trish speaking."

"Hi, Babe. What's happening?"

"Oh, Dad!" Trish swallowed past the boulder that had suddenly lodged in her throat at the sound of the familiar voice. "How did you know how much I needed you?"

"Hey, we've always said great minds run in the same circles." Her father's voice rasped from a throat raw from coughing. "Now what's our great minds' problem?"

"It's the gray filly. When I went back out to last-check the stock, she was down. Caesar and I—no, *God*, Caesar and I got her up and into the barn. Her temp was 104."

"Slow down. Slow down. Why don't you call the vet, then call me back. Then you can tell me what you mean by God, Caesar and you. Sounds like a good story." He paused, his voice deepening, reassuring his daughter. "Take it easy, Trish. Everything's going to be all right."

"Thanks, Dad." Trish forced her hand on the receiver to relax. "I'll get right back to you."

Amazing, Trish thought when the phone at the vet's was answered on the first ring.

"Bradshaw here."

"I'm so glad you're home. This is Trish from Runnin' On Farm. I've got a yearling filly with a temp of 104. She was down, sweaty and shivery. She didn't want to get up."

"First, get her up into the barn."

"I've already done that."

"Good, good. I'll be there in about fifteen minutes."

"Thanks, Doc."

"Oh . . . and Trish?"

"Yeah?"

"Sorry to hear about your dad."

Boy, news sure travels fast, Trish thought as she said thanks and hung up the phone. Then she turned the yellow pages for hospitals. *Ah, St. Joseph's.* She wrote the number on a pad by the phone.

"Hal Evanston's room, please," she responded to the operator.

"That's room 731. I'll ring it for you."

"Thanks." Trish scribbled the number down by the other as she switched the receiver to her other ear. "Dad?" Trish leaped in before the hoarse "hello."

"Yes, Trish. What did you find out?"

"He's coming right over."

"Good."

"You don't sound so good." Trish cradled the phone on her shoulder while she pushed up to sit on the kitchen counter. "Been coughing again?"

Her father chuckled, carefully. "Can't get away with much around you, can I? Forget that for now. What's going on around there, and what's this about God and Caesar helping you?"

By the time Trish finished describing the incident of the nip on the rump, Hal laughed until a coughing spell took his breath away.

"Sorry, Tee. But that was a good one. 'Please God'— and Caesar bites her on the rump." He chuckled more carefully this time. "Guess I don't have to worry about you at all. You, God and Caesar. What a combination!"

Trish giggled in return. "You be good now. No matter what, we need you around here. Next time Caesar might tune out his heavenly hearing."

"No chance. His ears are perfect. You just keep on praying, that'll do it."

"Thanks, Dad." She gripped the phone like it was the lifeline connecting her to safety. "I gotta get back to the barn. Talk to you later."

"I'll call you. The switchboard won't let calls through after nine. They think we patients need our beauty sleep." He snorted. "As if beauty sleep would do me any good at this stage in my life."

"Hey, is Mom still there?"

"No, she and David left just before you called. They were stopping for hamburgers and then groceries. What do you need?"

"Nothing. Talk to you later." Trish breathed a sigh of relief when she hung up the phone. She wasn't sure what she'd been expecting, but he sounded good, she thought. *Except for that awful coughing.*

The headlights from the traveling veterinary clinic

flashed in her eyes as she opened the gate. By the time the vet had parked the pick-up and stepped out, Trish had run the distance to the barns.

"This way, Dr. Bradshaw. I've cross-tied her in the isolation box."

The grizzle-haired man quickly unlocked the rear boxes. "Let me get my gear. Sounds to me like you've got everything under control." As he talked, he chose syringes, bottles and gloves and laid them in a stainless steel bucket. "You've got hot water?" He pulled on his galoshes.

Trish wished she could find the button to shift the deliberate man from low to high gear.

All the horses nickered, their curious faces hanging over the stall doors. Spitfire tossed his head and kicked the wall.

"Later, fella." Trish didn't even take time for one ear rub.

"They all look alert," the vet said. "Good sign."

"So far it's just the filly." Trish paused. "Oh, and maybe one of the brood mares. I'd like you to check her before you leave."

"Sure enough." They opened the stall door. The gray filly didn't even raise her head. She leaned against the ropes, seeming to depend on them for stability.

Trish held the animal's head up while Dr. Bradshaw checked eyes, ears, nose and throat. A hush fell over the stall, as he placed his stethoscope against the filly's heaving ribs.

Make it something simple, God, Trish prayed in the silence of her mind. *So he can give her a shot and make her all better.*

I prayed that for Dad too, she thought, *and look what*

happened. He's in the hospital. And cancer sure isn't simple. She rubbed her forehead against the filly's soft cheek. *And there're no shots to cure cancer.*

"This time a shot or two will do," she whispered into the droopy ear. "I know it will."

"Well," the vet said as he removed the stethoscope and patted the gray rump. "Looks like a virus to me. I'll load her up with antibiotics to prevent any secondary infection, but the only cure is good care. And time. You've got to keep her eating and drinking. Especially drinking. So far, the ones I've seen respond pretty quickly when I catch them as early as this. The real problem comes if they go into pneumonia."

Trish felt the weight fall off her shoulders. "I'll watch her."

"Make sure you don't contaminate the other horses. This stuff is highly contagious. Don't even go into their stalls with boots you've worn in this stall. Here, wash your hands before we go check that mare. Can you give injections?" he asked as he scrubbed his hands in the disinfectant water.

"Yes. Dad made me practice. Said every horsewoman had better be able to doctor her own stock."

"Good. Good." Dr. Bradshaw patted her shoulder, his hand accustomed to conveying comfort. "I'll leave this bottle. You've got disposable syringes?"

"Sure, in the tack room."

"Give her fifteen cc's both morning and night. Warm water to drink, and mix her grain with warm water and a little molasses. If she goes down on you, call me right away."

"Got it. Fifteen cc's."

The vet kept talking while he filled his syringe,

swabbed the filly's shoulder, and rammed the needle home. Trish gripped the halter extra hard, but the sick animal didn't even flinch.

When Trish unsnapped the tie ropes, the filly's head sank even lower. "I'll get some straw in here right away," Trish promised her with a last pat. "You hang in there."

Outside the stall, the vet removed his boots and stuck them in the bucket. "You keep a pair down here," he reminded her. "Do just like I'm doing."

"Okay. Will spraying the ones I have on with disinfectant take care of this evening?"

"I think so. But galoshes are better." He pulled a flashlight from his coverall pocket. "Let's go look at that mare."

When they reached the brood mares, everything seemed perfectly normal. All of them grazed peacefully, the sound of their munching drowned out by the singing frogs. Trish held each mare's head while the doctor listened to the horse's lungs with his stethoscope.

All was quiet. *Dumb horses*, Trish thought, *of course you won't cough while I have someone here to help you*.

"Can't hear a thing." Bradshaw took back the flashlight he'd given Trish to hold. "But watch them carefully. As I said, that stuff's pretty contagious. Call me if you see or hear anything unusual."

By the time the vet had reloaded his gear and reminded Trish of all his instructions, two sets of headlights turned into the farm gate.

"Looks like you have company." He shut his door.

"Mom and David are just getting home from town. Thanks for coming so quickly. I really appreciate it."

"Any time, Trish. See you." The doctor honked his horn and waved as the incoming cars braked in the gravel.

"What's Bradshaw doing here?" David slammed his car door.

"The gray filly has a virus. He says it's really contagious so we have to be extra careful."

"Oh great," David groaned, "that's all we need."

"I'll be up in a minute. Just gotta fork some straw in her stall and get her a bucket of warm water."

"Want me to do it?"

"Naw, my boots are already contaminated. Won't take me long."

"Trish." Dave stopped her. "Better be prepared. Mom's pretty upset."

"About Dad?"

"That . . . and other things."

By other things, he means me, Trish thought as she loped back to the barn. *So what's new?*

CHAPTER 7

Fifteen minutes later, Trish slid open the glass door and sank into the nearest chair. At the staccato tap of her mother's heels, Trish looked up.

Her "Hi, Mom" trailed into a whisper when she noticed the white line around her mother's tight mouth. With a clenched jaw and hands to match, her mother stopped two feet in front of her.

"I thought you cared about your father, but it's just like I've always said. Those horses come first in your life."

The attack left Trish in a momentary state of shock. "But, Mom." She shook her head, as if to clear her ears. "Someone had to do the chores. You know Dad always says—"

"You listen to me for a change." Marge's words were clipped, each syllable sliced as if with a sharp knife. "Your father is more important to me than anything on this earth. The horses, the racing—I don't care about those. When he asked for you tonight, where were you?"

"But—" Trish was frantic to get a word in.

"I've had it!" Her mother turned toward the living room. She shook her head. "I've just had it with you, Tricia."

"But, Mom!" Trish bit off the plea.

"Horses. All the time! Sometimes I hate those animals."

"That's not fair." Trish leaped to their defense.

"You were needed somewhere else—where were you?"

"Mom! David went with you. Somebody had to take care of things around here." Trish tore her fingers through her hair. "The filly went down and—"

"Mother . . . Trish!" David vainly tried to interrupt.

"Do you think Dad wants everything to fall apart around here?" Trish's voice rose. "He's sick enough, and all you're worried about is whether or not I went to the hospital. Well, you can worry all you want to, because I *couldn't* go tonight." She brushed away the tears cascading down her cheeks. "And I probably won't go tomorrow either."

"That's nothing new. When have you ever done what I wanted?" her mother countered.

"Well, Mom, if I did what you wanted, we wouldn't have a jockey to race this year." The rage welled up within her like a mushroom cloud. "You never want me to do the things I like best. I'd rather be with horses than with people any day!"

"Tricia!" her mother reprimanded.

"You started this, Mother. Dad and I love racing."

"That's fine for a man. But in case you haven't figured it out yet, you're fast becoming a woman. Racing thoroughbreds is a man's job."

"No! No, it's not! You know there are women jockeys. And they do okay. You just worry all the time. You don't want your daughter to be different." The feelings of rebellion within scared her but she couldn't stop the flood of words. "Remember, you've said, 'always tell the truth.' Well the truth is, when it comes to racing, I *don't care* if you don't agree with me!"

"Watch your mouth, young lady!"

"I have a right to say what I think!"

"Trish, go to your room." Her mother took a step closer. "I'll not allow you to talk to me like that."

"You can't stand the truth, can you? When you don't like what I have to say you send me to my room. Maybe I should sleep in the stable!"

"Tricia Evanston!"

"I don't care. Anyplace is better than here." Trish glared through her tears at her mother, then stomped down the hall. The slam of her door echoed through the house.

With a grunt she pulled off her boots and heaved them one after the other against the closet door. The tears blinded her eyes and caught in her throat. If only kicking and screaming would help.

I hate her! her mind screamed. She threw herself across the bed and sobbed. *And I know she hates me. After all I did tonight to help, and she just rips into me. Those horses are our business—Dad's and mine.* The tears raised blotches on her face and soaked circles on her bed. *I'd be better off at the track. Maybe she'd be happier if I weren't here. But where would I go?* She tossed her head from side to side, as if to drum out the furious thoughts. *I hate her. I hate her.*

Her mind went numb. The word hate echoed in the dark corridors of her brain. *Hate. I hate crying. I hate fighting. Oh God, why are things so messed up? I need my Dad! You say You love us but Dad's so sick; Mom's yelling at me . . . none of this feels like love.*

She gulped down another sob. With one hand she fumbled for a tissue on the nightstand. Tears and nose-blowing soaked that one and the next.

"Trish." David knocked softly on her door.

"What."

"Can I come in?"

"Oh, why not?" She sat up on the edge of the bed, blew her nose again and mopped her eyes.

"Don't ask me to apologize." She hunched her shoulders, her face hidden in her hands. "Not this time. She started it." Trish could feel the tears clogging her throat again.

David sat beside her on the bed. "Yeah, I know." He rested his elbows on his knees. "But Tee, things have been awfully rough on her today."

"Sure. And my day's been wonderful? Why'd she have to take it out on me?"

"She really felt we all needed to be together as a family, to give Dad all of our support." He handed her another tissue.

"Somebody had to be here, to keep things going."

"That's true. But if you'd gone in for just a little while—"

"I *can't* go in there." Trish buried her whisper in her fingers.

"What do you mean, you *can't* go in there?" David leaned forward, his hands clasped between his knees.

"I can't. That's what I mean." She fell back on the bed, the back of her hand hiding her eyes.

David stared at her, confusion wrinkling his brow. "Well, if you don't make any more sense than that, how can you expect Mom or anyone else to understand?"

"I don't know." Trish's voice sounded like it came from the closet, far away. "All I know is that I just can't go in there." The silence stretched. "And I hate fighting." She sniffed. "I always feel so guilty afterward, like everything in the whole world is all my fault."

"Then go say you're sorry."

"I hate that most of all." She hiccupped. "Besides, this time it was *not* my fault."

"Tee."

"Well . . ." She could feel the thoughts whipping around her brain like a gerbil on a wheel. A knock at the door brought the wheel to an abrupt stop.

"Trish." Her mother's voice came softly through the door.

"Yeah."

"Can I come in?"

"I guess."

David squeezed her hand.

"Trish—" Marge joined her children on the edge of the bed, three sets of jean-clad knees pressed together. "Please forgive me for unloading on you like that. It was totally inexcusable." She shook her head. "I know you had a terrible day too."

Wordlessly Trish nodded, tears brimming in her green eyes again. When she could look at her mother, she saw tears that matched her own. "I'm sorry, too," she whispered. "I hate fighting."

Marge wrapped both arms around her daughter and held her close. "Oh, Trish. I love you so."

Trish felt the steady thumping of her mother's heart. She nestled closer, feeling safe within those protecting arms. Her mother's sweet perfume was somehow an added comfort. "I always say stuff I don't want to when I'm mad." Trish raised her face.

Marge wiped the tears from her daughter's cheek. "I know. We all do." She drew in a deep breath. "How about if I forgive you and you forgive me and we go on from here?"

Trish nodded. "Thanks, Mom."

Both reached for the tissues at the same time.

"Now," her mother went on, "how about the animals? You said you were having a problem."

"Oh, dear!" Trish leaped to her feet. "Dad never called back about the filly. I should call him."

David looked at his watch. "You can try, but it's nearly 11:00." David gave his sister a push out of the room. "So, go call him."

Just as she reached the phone it rang. Trish jumped liked she'd touched a live wire instead of a phone. "Runnin' On Farm." She tried to sound business-like instead of breathless. "Dad! The phone rang just as I touched it. Spooky."

"As I've said, great minds . . ."

"Yeah, same circles. How are you?"

"Could be better, but the real question is how's the filly?"

"Well, Dr. Bradshaw shot her full of antibiotics and said to keep her isolated. I'm to give her fifteen cc's more morning and night for the next couple of days."

"How does she look?"

"Droopy—but the doc said the ones he's treated early like this respond pretty fast."

"What about the rest of the stock?"

"He checked the brood mares and the two colts. All clear, but I have to keep a close eye on everything." Trish cupped the phone on her shoulder as she leaned her elbows on the counter.

"How's your mother?"

"Well," Trish paused to chew her lip. "We're okay . . . now."

"Been fighting again?"

Trish forced her voice to remain calm. "Don't worry about us, Dad. Just take care of yourself." She drummed her fingers on the counter. "Hey, you know what? I have

to wear galoshes when I treat the filly. Think what I'll
look like in your giant-sized boots. I could put both feet
in one and still have room."

"Tee, you nut."

"I'll look nutty, alright. Just call me hoppity."

"Okay, Peter Cottontail, back to the filly." Trish could
feel his warm smile over the wire. "Where do you have
her?"

"In the isolation stall, where else?" Surprise at his
question raised her eyebrows.

"Sorry," her father sounded sheepish. "I should have
known you'd do exactly the right thing."

"You taught me, Dad." Trish hugged the phone closer
to her ear, as if the action would bring him closer to her.
"That's why I have to wear the galoshes, to keep from
contaminating the others. I'll check on her now, before
I go to bed."

"Tee, I'm proud of you. But let David check her during
the night. He can do the chores in the morning too.
You've got to get to school on time for a change."

"Dad . . ."

"You heard me. You can work Spitfire on the starting
gates in the afternoon. And David can . . . let me talk to
David. You get to bed."

"But what about Spitfire's morning workout?"

"Okay. Gallop him four miles like you've been doing.
But leave the rest for David."

"Yes, sir." Trish swallowed a lump in her throat. "And
please get better, Dad."

"Keep praying, Babe. All of us have to keep praying."

"I'll get David." She laid the phone down on the
counter and rubbed her hand across her face.

After David picked up the receiver, Trish slid the door
open and stepped outside. Caesar whined for attention,

then shoved his cold nose into her hand. She scratched behind his ears, all the while concentrating on her prayer. *God, make my Dad better. Bring him home to us, to me. He's a good person and he loves You. Please make him all right again.*

All the way to the barn *Please, God!* ran over and over in her brain. Soft nickers snapped her back to the present when she reached the stable. Quietly she opened the tack room door and felt on the shelf for the flashlight. The light helped her find the galoshes and slide her wet sneakers into the huge boots. They came nearly to her knees. To keep them from falling off, she shuffled her feet down the row to the filly's stall.

The filly lay asleep in the straw, breathing heavily but no longer shivering. Trish flashed the light into the half-empty bucket.

"Good, girl," she whispered as she stooped and ran her hand down the animal's neck. The filly just flicked her ears. "I'll get you another bucket. Drink lots."

By the time Trish's head hit the pillow, the numbers on her digital clock had flipped over 12:00. She set her alarm for 5:30 and snuggled down under the covers.

Oh, no! she sighed deeply, feeling it through her whole weary body. *My chemistry—and that essay is due by three.* Like a swallow swooping through the spring sunshine, the thought of getting up and studying flitted through her mind and flew away again.

Tomorrow. I'll catch up tomorrow.

CHAPTER 8

Dawn hadn't cracked the darkness yet.

Trish squashed her pillow over her ears at the buzzer. She hit the snooze button and jumped when the alarm rang again. Five minutes extra sleep was not long enough, she needed five hours more, at least.

By the time she'd pulled on her jeans and sweatshirt and fumbled for her boots, David tapped on her door.

"You about ready?" His tone didn't sound any livelier than she felt.

"Yeah." She ran her fingers through her hair. The hairdresser called it finger-combing. Trish called it sheer desperation. "Gotta spray these boots first," she said as she came out of her bedroom.

She grabbed the disinfectant spray from under the kitchen sink, her down vest off the hook, and met David on the deck. "Why don't you feed and I'll start working Spitfire." She looked up from dowsing her boots. "That way maybe I'll have time to do something else."

"Remember, Dad said school on time today."

Trish wrinkled her nose. "I know. If I could just take a leave of absence or something." She wiped her nose with the back of her hand. "Phew, that stuff *smells* bad enough to kill germs." She pulled her boots on and with

Caesar trotting beside them, they jogged down to the barns.

The eastern skyline glowed a faint lemon yellow, but overhead the stars still shone valiantly, fighting off their moment of demise.

"Going to be a nice day." Trish filled her lungs with the crisp air. "Sure wish I could stay home."

"Knock it off." David swatted her behind. "I'll help you mount up. If we hustle, you can work Firefly too. I'll have her saddled so if you're on your way to the house at 7:00, you should be okay. Mom said she'd drop you off at school on her way to the hospital."

"She's going that early?" Trish bridled Spitfire, ignoring the nickerings on down the line. "Stop that." She slapped the horse smartly when he reached around and nipped her shoulder. "Have to keep an eye on you every minute," she muttered. "Good thing you just got my vest."

David boosted her into the saddle and waited while she gathered up her reins. "Now, you know what Dad said."

"David," she tapped him on the head with her whip. "You make a lousy mother hen. Besides, one mother is enough." Trish loosed the reins enough for Spitfire to crow-hop once before he jigged sideways to the entry to the track. She turned him to the left, clockwise, and kept a tight hold on his mouth. Her father had taught her well. *No matter how much of a hurry you're in, never—but never, cheat on the warm-up time.* Strained muscles were too easily come by and too costly to cure.

After several laps at the restricted pace, Spitfire was warmed up, both from the easy gait and from fighting for his freedom every step of the way. Trish knew she'd been having a workout. Who needed free weights when she had Spitfire?

The long, slow gallop that built endurance wasn't any more to his liking. Finally, she pulled him down to a walk. "Listen, horse. Just settle down." She rubbed his neck, high on the crest and under his sweaty mane. "You know the routine as well as I do, so behave yourself. There'll be no racing today." Spitfire snorted as if in answer. "I don't care what you think. Those are Dad's orders. Now let's try this again. Slow gallop, you hear me?" The horse's ears twitched back and forth, both listening to her and checking out everything in the area.

Trish walked a final circuit, took him back to the barn and repeated the process with Firefly. Temperament-wise, she was the exact opposite of her half-brother. Trish could relax more around her; the dark bay filly was always eager to please her rider instead of fighting her way around the track.

Trish slid off the sweaty filly at the end of the work-out, threw the reins at David and dashed up to the house. "Don't forget the shot for the sick filly." She back-pedaled as she shouted instructions to David. "Fifteen cc's and watch her." It was 7:10.

No matter how she hurried, she couldn't make up that ten minutes. The frown on her mother's face as they backed the car out of the garage at 7:55 clouded the ten-minute drive to Prairie High.

"I'm not writing an excuse." Marge checked both ways before they pulled out onto the road.

"Fine," Trish mumbled around her mouthful of peanut butter toast. *Don't bother,* she thought. *If I have to stay after to make up these tardy times, I'll just have to stay after. They're lucky I'm making it to school at all.*

"You know your main responsibility is school and your schoolwork, Tricia," her mother reminded her.

Trish cringed. Her schoolwork. She'd really have to make better use of study hall than she had. Maybe David would have time tonight to help her with her chemistry. All the rest she could manage. She'd write that essay during history and—

"How far behind are you?" Marge's jaw had that iron look.

Trish started to say, "I'm fine," but a look at her mother's face made her mumble, "not too bad."

"What's not too bad?"

"I'll catch up today," Trish stated flatly. "Don't worry about my schoolwork."

"Trish . . ." Marge laid her hand on her daughter's knee.

"Don't worry." Trish jumped from the car as soon as it stopped at the curb. She leaned back in, "Tell Dad 'Hi' for me," and loped away, her books caught under one arm.

The stop at the office made Trish more uncomfortable.

"Where's your excuse slip?" The receptionist glanced up at the clock. "You're seven minutes late."

"I know." Trish chewed her lip, the desire to tell just a tiny fib uppermost in her mind. She shrugged. "I took too long at the barn and Mom refused to write me an excuse. I'd promised her I wouldn't be late again."

"You know this goes on your record?" The woman signed the small pink slip and handed it over the counter.

"I know. Thanks." Trish felt like tearing up the piece of paper but knew she wouldn't get into class without it. She slammed her fist against her locker when it wouldn't open on the first attempt. *Boy,* she thought as she dashed across the quad, *this day is really gonna be a great one.*

Trish used every spare minute, and by lunch time had even made up one chemistry assignment. Her essay was ready to recopy. She debated skipping lunch but her stomach reminded her that breakfast had been less than filling.

"How's your Dad?" Rhonda asked as they joined the lunch line.

"He sounded pretty good on the phone last night." Trish glanced around the noisy room. "Have you seen Doug?"

"You going to the after-game party with him?"

"No. I won't be going at all."

"Won't be going where?" Brad joined their slow shuffle to the counter.

"To the party," Rhonda answered for her friend. "Tee, how can we help? I know you've got tons to do."

"Well, you could tell Doug I've got mono or something. He'll ask me why I can't go and I hate telling people about my Dad." Trish hunched her shoulders. She hadn't let herself think about her father and the hospital this morning. Yesterday had been overwhelming, today she had regained some of her control. Fear that her mother might carry out the no-racing-threat made her concentrate on her homework. The last thing she needed was an I-told-you-so from her mother. She *would* manage—somehow.

Rhonda snapped her fingers in front of Trish's eyes. "Hey, Trish, come back. What do you want for lunch?"

"Uh-h, tuna salad, milk and an apple." She spotted Doug waving at her from a table in the back. She made a face at Rhonda, paid for her lunch and carried her tray to the seat Doug had saved for her.

"Hi." Her smile felt like it was stuck on with Elmer's glue.

"Hi, yourself." He pushed his books out of the way to make room for her.

"Doug, I'd love to go to the party with you, but I can't," she blurted. "I need every minute to train for the Meadows and staying out late—well, you know how it is."

"Sounds like your coach is as tough as mine."

"Tougher. We have a lot of money tied up in these races."

"Yeah, I know." Doug nodded. "Maybe some other time?"

"Sure. After the season. It ends in April." Trish drained her milk. "I gotta rewrite this paper. Thanks for asking me." She stuffed the apple in her purse and rose to take her tray back.

Doug put his hand on her arm. "I'll do that." He looked up at her, his smile wide as the skies. "See you in the winner's circle. We'll all be there to watch your race."

Trish swallowed another lump that clogged her throat. *He is so cool.* "Thanks."

Trish found a bench outside in the sun and began the rewrite. She corrected a couple of sentences, trying to keep her handwriting legible but still writing as fast as possible. Generally she liked writing. She'd even thought about getting on the school paper staff, but as usual there was no time.

The bell rang, but she only had one more side to copy.

"There'll be a quiz tomorrow," the chemistry teacher announced just as the bell rang. "So be prepared. Remember, quizzes total twenty-five percent of your final grade." The groans from thirty students would have done justice to an announcement of thirty days hard labor, Trish's included. That was all she needed.

Brad was waiting for her as she came out of her last class. "You want a ride?"

Trish nodded. "Thanks. Let me get my stuff out of my locker."

"How'd it go?" Rhonda asked as Trish opened the car door.

"How'd what go?"

"With Doug." Rhonda's look suggested Trish had lost her marbles.

"He understood. Just told him I couldn't break training." Trish slammed the door as she settled herself in the front seat.

"Good thinking." Rhonda leaned forward and patted Trish on the shoulder. "Hey, you need any help this afternoon?"

"Probably. Who know's how much David got done."

"We'll be right over then, won't we Brad?"

"Yup. Maybe today I'll get promoted to exercise boy on a permanent basis." Brad grinned at Trish. "Rhonda can muck out the stalls."

"Thanks, buddy," came from the back seat. "I'm not the one who needs bigger biceps."

Warm from the laughter of her friends, Trish didn't mind the empty house quite as much. Besides, David's car in the driveway assured her someone was home. The phone rang just as she was heading out the door to the stables, peanut butter and jelly sandwich in hand.

A stranger's voice answered her business-like response. "May I speak to Hal Evanston, please."

"I'm sorry, he's not here right now," Trish answered. "Can I help you?"

"This is John Carter. I have two thoroughbreds and a quarterhorse I want trained and conditioned for the track. I know I'm late getting started but I just purchased the one. A couple of people at The Meadows recommended Hal. Could you have him get back to me?"

"Sure will," Trish answered. "What's your number, Mr. Carter?"

Dollar signs played tag in her head as Trish ran down to the barn. She found David and Caesar out with the mares. "David," she called as she reached the gate, "guess what?"

"Get me another lead shank, will you?" He was leading the brood mare who'd been coughing the afternoon before.

"She's worse?"

"I think so. We'll take 'em all up and check temps. That's the only way to be sure."

Where are we gonna put more sick horses? Trish's mind raced as fast as her feet. *Guess we better clean out the old barn. They'd be isolated over there all right.*

Brad and Rhonda met them at the barn. Trish had one mare and David the two others. One of them coughed again.

"Looks like you need help for sure." Brad took the lead ropes. "Where do you want them tied?"

"Bradshaw said we have to keep them isolated, so how about the old barn?" Trish looked at David for confirmation. At his nod, she continued. "Rhonda, grab the wheelbarrow and throw in a couple of forks. We'll have to clean those old stalls out. Brad, tie those two to the outside rings and I'll get some straw after I take this one down." She rubbed the coughing mare's nose. "Pregnant as you are, you don't need to be sick too."

"When's she due? "Brad asked as they led the animals out.

"Around the twentieth, I think." Trish rubbed the mare's neck as they walked. "I keep telling Dad that if she foals on my birthday, the foal should be mine."

"Sounds good to me," Brad agreed.

They tied the animals up. While David checked temperatures, Trish helped Rhonda with the cleaning gear.

"We better call Bradshaw," David said when he came into the dim barn. "One temp with those three, and I think another of the yearlings is coming down with it. He wasn't kidding when he said it was contagious."

How do we keep the racing stock safe? Trish thought as she dog-trotted back up to the house to call the vet. *We've got to be able to move Spitfire and the others to the track next week.*

CHAPTER 9

The phone was ringing as Trish came through the door.

"Runnin' On Farm," she panted. "Trish speaking." She paused and smiled at the response. "Hi, Mom. No, David's down at the barn. We've got a couple more sick ones. I just came up to call the vet. How's Dad?"

"He's in the recovery room," her mother answered. "They did the bronchoscopy about an hour ago. How about you and David meeting me here at the hospital for dinner and then you can visit with your dad for a while?"

"I don't know." Trish felt caught in a trap. "I told you the mare is sick, and so is another yearling. Even with Rhonda and Brad helping, it'll take several hours to prep stalls."

"Where are you putting them?"

"Down in the old barn." At the silence in her ear, Trish swallowed. "We're doing everything we can and . . ."

"Yes, I know." Marge bit off each word. "The horses always come first. But not if your presence here could help make your father feel better."

"Tell Dad I'll call him later . . . when we know more." The line went dead without a goodbye. Why couldn't David have been the one to talk with her? *He always*

77

manages to make things better, Trish thought. *I just make it worse.*

She called the vet and left a message for Dr. Bradshaw to come as soon as possible. Her chemistry book stared up at her accusingly from where she'd dropped it on the counter. She gave it a push. *Somewhere I'll find the time to study.* Her feet dragged on the way back to the stable. She hadn't told David about the Carter phone call. Fat chance they had of taking on any more horses now.

"I left a message on his machine." Trish found David bringing up the other two yearlings. "And Mom wants you to call her. She asked us to come in for dinner. I told her what's going on."

"And . . ."

"She wasn't very happy. Don't blame her, I'm not either."

David tied the two colts to the outside rings. "Why don't you go work Anderson's two. The three of us will get this place in shape. Dad said to put Brad on the payroll again so we can count on the extra help."

"How's the filly?"

"About the same. At least she's drinking."

"I'll call when I need a leg-up. Those four been out on the hot walker today?" She nodded toward the horses they'd been training.

"Yup. Be careful with that hellion."

"What'd he do now?" Trish knew immediately that Dave meant the Anderson colt, Gatesby.

"He sure spooks easy."

"I know."

"Be careful."

"Yes, mother hen." Trish laughed as she evaded her brother's swat.

Always one to get the worst out of the way first, Trish cross-tied Gatesby in his stall, brushed him down, then bridled and saddled him. He stood, docile for a change, with only his ears responding to her soft monologue. Trish knew he behaved better for her than anyone, but he sure was a handful. And today they should be training him at the starting gate. Time was running out on getting him ready for the first part of the season.

Brad gave her a leg-up when she called for help. The colt just stood there until Trish was settled and she clucked him off. He set out for the track in a flat-footed walk, looking around him with only mild interest.

Trish waved her thanks and concentrated on the warm-up. The entire session, even to walking him around the gates, only drew some snorting and eye-rolling on the colt's part. She patted his neck and smoothed his mane down as they stood a few feet from the starting gates. *That metal monster would be enough to scare anyone,* she thought. *Wait till he's boxed in with gates closed in behind and in front of him.* She rubbed the horse's neck again and turned him toward the stable.

"We'll work you with Dan'l tomorrow," she said as he twitched his ears. "All of us will be at the gate at once. That should make things easier."

The sun had set by the time she finished working Anderson's three-year-old. He'd already raced one season and was being reconditioned after an injury during the summer program in Spokane. He was a willing animal, without the contrariness of Gatesby. Trish breezed him twice around the track for the pure joy of running.

She scraped him down and rinsed the sweat off with warm water. Brad had taken care of Gatesby, so with both animals snapped to the hot walker to cool off, Trish spent a moment with old Dan'l.

"Tomorrow you get to train the kids." She rubbed his head, right behind his ears, a favorite place. "Hope they watch you and learn fast." Dan'l rubbed his nose against her chest and blew softly in her face.

For a moment Trish could pretend everything was all right. Her father was working in one of the other stalls; the exerciser sang its creaky song, and all the animals were healthy. Her mom was up baking cookies and soon dinner would be on the table.

"Where do you have the sick ones now, Trish?" Doctor Bradshaw's question broke her reverie.

She swallowed as she turned away from Dan'l and her dream. "Down at the old barn. I'll show you."

The mercury yardlight had come on before they had all the sick animals in separate clean stalls and the racing stock exercised. Training had been minimal, compared to what Trish knew needed to be done.

"How's your dad?" Rhonda asked as they trudged up the rise to the cars.

"Not coming home right away," Trish sighed.

"Are you going in to the hospital tonight?"

"No, it's too late." Trish kicked a small rock ahead of her, the action slowing her steps so David and Brad pulled ahead.

"That why your mom's mad?" Rhonda stopped beside her friend.

"Yup. She can't understand why I haven't gone to visit my dad."

"Well, why haven't you?"

"I don't know." Trish searched for words to explain her feelings. "I just can't go in there. It's like . . . well . . . if I go there . . ."

Rhonda waited out the silence.

Trish shook her head. "Rhonda, I'm so scared. I'm just so scared." She kicked another rock, viciously this time. "What if he dies?" Tears spilled over. She dashed a hand across her eyes and shook her head again. "I just can't go to the hospital. Dad *has* to come home."

————

By the time Trish opened her chemistry book that night, she was so tired she could hardly read the print. She took her book into the living room. "David, can you help me with this stuff?"

David was sound asleep on the sofa; his half-eaten sandwich on a plate on the floor. Trish threw the afghan over him and went back to her desk.

An hour later Marge found her daughter, head on her chemistry book, fast asleep. "Trish," she shook her gently. "You better get to bed."

Trish felt like she was crawling up out of a deep hole. "Hi, Mom." She blinked and turned in her chair. "How's Dad?"

"We have some good news. After his radiation treatment tomorrow, I may be able to bring him home. They started with chemotherapy today, so it depends on how he's feeling."

Trish spoke out of her fog. "He's better then?"

"Well, we just have to pray the treatments help. We'll know more in a couple of weeks. Tonight he was pretty sleepy from the anesthetic and the medication."

And you didn't even call him, Trish's conscience scolded. *What kind of daughter am I?* she thought. *Maybe Mom was right about wondering how much I love Dad.* She swallowed against the lump that seemed to be making itself at home right behind her tonsils.

"You better get to bed." Marge rubbed Trish's tight shoulders.

"I have a quiz tomorrow. Gotta study some more." Trish stared at the sparsely filled paper glaring up at her. Three problems done out of ten. Big deal. And she had one more assignment after that. And review for a quiz. None of the stuff made any sense anyway.

"Let David take care of things in the morning. You sleep in," her mother suggested.

"Maybe." Trish picked up her pencil. *Why not have David do my chemistry and I'll work the horses?* she thought. Made a lot more sense. *Oh sure, and he could take the quiz too,* her nagging inner voice jumped back into the act. Trish looked longingly at her bed. Just one more hour. Surely she could study one more hour.

She flunked her chemistry quiz. The score stood one out of ten. Trish stared at the paper in her hand. She'd never flunked anything before. What if her mother asked how the quiz went? She stuffed the paper into her folder and tried to pay attention to the lecture. All those symbols, how would she ever get them all memorized?

Trish had a hard time paying attention all day. Good thing it was Friday. She'd be able to catch up over the weekend. When the last bell rang, she bolted for Brad's car. Give her the horses and track any day.

"Where's Rhonda?" she asked as she slid into the front seat.

"Her mom picked her up so they could leave early for the show this weekend." Brad backed out of his parking place.

"Sure wish I could be there for her. Those are nearly professional jumping classes she's entered. She's up against the big time."

"Be nice if we could all be there." Brad patted her knee. "But don't worry, Rhonda understands."

"I know," Trish sighed. *I just wish I understood,* she thought. *Everything is so messed up. Maybe . . .* her thoughts brightened. *Just maybe Dad will be there when I get home.*

He wasn't. No one was. A scrawled note from David said he'd gone to the hospital to see Dad. He'd be back around four.

"Well, that's great," Trish muttered as she changed her clothes. "You could at least have told me what needs to be done." She gathered up a load of dirty jeans and stuffed them into the washing machine. "No one ever tells me anything around here." She poured a glass of milk, stared longingly at the empty cookie jar and grabbed an apple. Slamming the sliding glass door took skill, but she managed.

Clouds covered the sun, the gray light matching her mood. Even the horses seemed subdued as she and Caesar approached the barn. Spitfire only nickered. She missed the sound of his hoof slamming the wall.

What if they're all coming down with the virus? She stalked from stall to stall, checking each of the horses in training. They all seemed fine, just dozing. Relief, like water from a hose, washed over her.

She hugged Dan'l, comfort stealing into her bones as he nibbled at her hair. "You guys are all just lazy." She rubbed his ears and smoothed the coarse gray mane. "Wish I had time to ride you today. But you can play teacher with Brad or David to our trainees. How about showing them all you know?"

By the time she had Dan'l and Spitfire groomed and saddled, David and Brad drove up one after the other. Trish left the two animals cross-tied and began on Anderson's three-year-old. Gatesby would have to wait for her. She patted his nose as she went by, only to get a wall-eyed snort in response.

"On second thought." She grabbed a lead rope and snapped it to his halter. "I'll let you work off some of that orneriness on the hot walker."

"Good idea." Brad watched with her a moment as the colt struck out at imaginary shadows with his forefeet, shaking his head at the confining rope.

"How's Dad?" Trish asked as David loped up. "Is he coming home today?"

David shook his head. "Maybe tomorrow. He was sleeping when I left."

"I'll call him as soon as we get back to the house."

David stared at her. "I told Mom I'd bring you in for a visit tonight."

"Well, you should have checked with me before you made any promises." Trish chewed her bottom lip. "I have too much to do."

"I don't understand you." David shook his head. His jawline matched his mother's now. "Well, let's get these guys going. I mucked out and brushed them all down this morning."

"How are the sickies?" Tricia asked as David boosted her into the saddle on Spitfire.

David left the stirrups long on Dan'l's saddle. "Here Brad, boost me up and then you take Dan'l," he said, settling himself on his horse before answering Tricia's question. "I think they're better. At least no worse, and the filly is eating again." Together they trotted toward the track. "Dad said to give these guys a good workout first, before we try the gate. We may put blinders on Gatesby and maybe even Spitfire."

Trish felt her low mood blowing away with the breeze in her face. Nothing gave her the high that working the thoroughbreds did. And if working them was this good, what would an actual race be like? Anticipation shivered down her spine.

———

"I can't believe it." Trish patted Spitfire's steaming black neck. "Good boy, you're fantastic." She felt like hugging the horse who had just walked flat-footed through the open starting gate. It was like playing Follow the Leader. Whatever Dan'l did, so did the others. They walked the horses through a couple more times before Brad dismounted and tied Dan'l to the track rail.

David gave him instructions as Trish brought Spitfire back to stop in the open gates. The colt rolled his eyes and tossed his head but remained standing as her comforting voice rippled past his ears.

When horse and rider entered the stall again, Brad had closed the front gate. Spitfire walked into the open-air stall and snorted at David's mount beside him.

"Okay," David said. "Let's put these two away and bring out the others. Brad, how about if you wash 'em down while Trish and I work Firefly and Gatesby? Then we'll use Dan'l again to teach them their lessons."

Trish felt an unfamiliar gnawing in her stomach at the thought of working Gatesby. He wasn't just unpredictable; sometimes he seemed deliberately mean. She shrugged it off as Brad boosted her into the saddle.

"Now you be careful with him." Brad kept a secure hand on the bridle. He walked them to the track. For a change, Gatesby seemed more interested in a workout than causing mischief.

Trish let the animal pick up his pace as he settled into the routine. Trot around once, then the long, conditioning slow-gallop. "If you just do this well at the gate, we'll call it a great day," Trish spoke into the twitching ears. After breezing him once around, she reined him into the center field beside Dan'l.

Gatesby didn't mind the gate. He rolled his eyes and tossed his head at the close enclosure but followed Dan'l on through. Firefly came right after him.

"Thank you, God." Trish murmured, grateful the tension she felt in her stomach hadn't made it through the reins to her mount. When Brad took hold of the bridle, she rubbed the bay's neck under his sweaty mane. "Good boy. You were super." She shook her head, beaming at Brad. "I can't believe it. Did you see that?"

"I know. That's the way I dreamed of it going, but I can't believe it either."

"Let's put 'em away while we're ahead." David walked his filly toward the track. "Tomorrow I'll move the starting gates out on the track. Since it's Saturday, we can take more time. If it goes like today, we'll be in great shape."

"I can't wait to tell Dad." Trish kicked her boots out of the stirrups and slid off the steaming horse. *He should have been here,* she thought as she unbuckled her saddle. *Heavenly Father, when are You going to bring him back to me?*

———

Trish felt like someone had socked her in the stomach after her call to the hospital. Her father could hardly talk. Once he'd had to throw-up while she waited. There were no jokes, and very little interest expressed in the horses.

"I'm sorry, Tee," his voice rasped just above a whisper. "You're doing a good job. I'll see you later."

"Right. Get well quick," Trish spoke into the dial tone after the receiver had bumped into its cradle.

What are they doing to him? She grabbed two TV dinners from the freezer and tossed them into the oven. *And they think I'm going in there—when he can't even talk on the phone?* She leaned over the sink, her stiff elbows supporting the crushing weight. *Dear God, what's happening to us? Where are You?*

CHAPTER 10

"I said I'm not going back to school. Not right now."

"Oh, David." Marge poured herself a cup of coffee.

Tricia stared at her brother. Why'd he want to ruin a Saturday morning by bringing up something like that? He knew Mom would lay into him, especially when she was still upset about last night. Trish could tell by the way her mother had avoided her.

Marge brought her coffee mug to the table and sat down. She rubbed her fingers across her forehead, as if to erase the lines gathering there.

"I was afraid you'd decide that." She shook her head. "But I hate for you to have to postpone your education."

"I know. But, Mom, it isn't forever. Maybe Dad'll be back on his feet in time for me to go back after Christmas. I'll be missing only one semester."

"Maybe." Marge ran her forefinger around the edge of her coffee mug.

"Besides, what else can we do? Those horses support us."

Trish felt like crying for David. She knew how much he had been looking forward to school again. His dream of veterinary medicine just got put on hold—for who knew how long, and he was talking about it so calmly. Mom was too. Amazing.

"I know." Marge sipped her coffee. "I've thought maybe I'd have to look for a job."

Trish unconsciously dropped her spoon into her empty cereal bowl.

The only other sound in the room was the bubbling fish tank.

"Well," Marge pushed her chair back. "I'd better get going. Maybe they'll let me bring Dad home today. Thanks, David." She squeezed his shoulder. "Trish, do you think there's any chance you can clean your room today?"

Trish felt the sarcasm bite. "I'll try."

"And maybe get some extra sleep—in your bed instead of on your desk?" Marge patted Trish's shoulder. "We don't need another sick one around here, and let's face it, you've been burning the candle at both ends and then some."

Grateful to be let off so easily, Trish just nodded.

"Brad will be over about ten," David said after their mother left the house. "Why don't you see what you can do about your bedroom between now and then? I'll get at the stalls and haul the gate onto the track."

"Okay." Trish drained her glass of milk. "David?"

"Yeah?"

"Things sure are a mess, aren't they." It was a statement, not a question.

———————

Trish glared at the disaster in her room. "Horses are more important any day," she muttered as she sorted the dirty clothes into one gigantic heap. She glared at a poster on her wall that said: "I'd rather be riding." After switching her wet jeans from the washer to the dryer, she dumped her shirts in the washer and went back to strip her bed. "Might as well do it right," she continued muttering to herself.

Within an hour, she had accomplished miracles. There was a floor there after all. By the time she vacuumed the carpet and hung up her newly washed clothes, she heard Brad's car in the driveway. "Well, at least Mom won't be able to holler at me for a messy room." Trish pulled on her boots and jogged down the slope, relieved to hear horses nickering instead of a vacuum cleaner roaring.

The three of them worked the horses in the same order as the day before. Since morning workouts had been done before breakfast, Trish put Spitfire into a slow gallop just twice around the track. He only snorted at the iron contraption taking up part of the dirt track and kept on at his easy gait.

They followed the same routine at the gates, too. Everyone paraded through after Dan'l. The old horse acted bored, his quietness calming the others.

Trish kept up her one-way conversations, all the words and cadence praising Spitfire for a fine performance.

"We'll close the rear gate," David said. "He's doing so well that we'll go ahead and release the front gate at the same time. You be ready, Trish. Let him get the feel of starting."

At David's signal the gate screeched closed. Both horses were penned on all sides. Trish felt Spitfire tremble. He laid back his ears but calmed as she talked to him, her hands steady on the reins.

"Okay, Brad." David spoke in a level voice. "Be ready, Trish."

As the gate clanged open, Trish loosed the reins and shouted. "Go, Spitfire."

Spitfire didn't need a second invitation. He bolted from the gate like a pro, running straight out within four strides. Trish stood in her stirrups to bring him back to a canter after they passed the second furlong post.

"Wow!" She turned him back toward the gate. "You are some fella."

"That was great." David cantered with her on the three-year-old. "Let's try it again, now that he knows what's going to happen."

They ran through the starting three more times and with each release, Spitfire smoothed out his strides. He entered the gates willingly, only his dancing front feet relaying his anticipation. Trish made him stop flat-footed before the gate released so that he'd get used to waiting in case another horse was cantankerous.

"Just wait till Dad sees you," she murmured into the flickering ears. "He'll be so proud of you."

They switched horses at the stable, unsnapping Gatesby from the exerciser. As if testing her mood, he nipped at Trish's shoulder. She jerked on the lead rope. The colt rolled his eyes but walked flat-footed beside her. Trish was careful to keep her feet well ahead of his. Gatesby made a practice of stepping on human toes.

Trish could hear her father's voice in her head: *You've got to watch him at all times. Gatesby's just not as careful with his feet as he should be.* Trish thought the bay was more intentional than careless. Somehow they had to break him of the nipping. If he was as persistent in winning as he was in being a pain, Gatesby could be a Derby winner.

When he trotted by the starting gate, Gatesby laid

his ears back and spooked to the side. Trish was prepared, her knees clamped and hands firm on the reins
as she pulled him back to a walk.

"Now, behave yourself," she scolded as she circled the
horse around the metal monster. When he quit snorting
she continued around the track, passing the gates several
times until the colt ignored them.

Gatesby followed Dan'l through with only a few
tosses of his head, but when the time came to stand with
the front gate closed, he reared at the screech. Trish
smacked him hard with the side of her fist, right between
his ears. "No!" she commanded at the same instant.
Gatesby dropped back to all fours and shook his head.

"Try it again." She had him reined down so tightly
his chin nearly touched his chest. When the gate
screeched closed, the horse quivered from ears to tail,
but he stood. Trish backed him out and walked him
around in a tight circle. "Let's get some grease on that
thing," she called to Brad. "It's the noise that's spooking
him."

She turned and trotted her mount around the track
until the guys were finished. This time Gatesby only
danced in place. Trish settled herself more firmly in the
saddle. "Okay, Brad, let's do it." As the gate swung open,
Trish loosed the reins and shouted, "Go!"

Gatesby paused only a fraction of a second before he
leaped at the command. He stumbled on the off forefoot
as he cleared the chute but regained his footing in a
stride and was running free.

Trish's grin, as she cantered him back to try again,
revealed her pleasure. "One more time, then try Dan'l
next to him."

Gatesby broke clean the second time and only

snorted when Dan'l walked into the stall next to him.

"Are you sure you don't want to quit while we're ahead?" David asked as he settled himself for the lunge.

"Race you two furlongs." Trish grinned over her shoulder. "He's plenty warm enough." She stroked the horse's sweaty neck with one gloved hand.

David hesitated. "You're on." He whispered to Dan'l's twitching ears, "Go for it, old man. When that gate opens, go for it."

Eyes straight ahead, Trish saw the gate swing and felt Gatesby lunge at the same instant. He nicked the gate. Stumbled. Tried to regain his footing. But before Trish could blink, the momentum from his lunge slammed them into the ground.

Trish could feel herself flying through the air, her reflexes commanding her to relax.

She tried.

"Tricia! Trish!"

She could hear the voice, but so faintly she wasn't sure where it was coming from.

"Call 911." She heard no more.

"Oh shoot," Trish mumbled as she pulled herself toward the circle of light somewhere above the black dungeon she floated in. The landscape paled like dawn breaking faint on the horizon. "We did it that time, didn't we?"

"Trish? Are you okay?"

"Yeah, Brad, I'll live." Trish opened her eyes. The light blurred on her goggles. She pushed them up, relieved to see the darkness was caused by dirt on the lenses. She spat some grit out of her mouth.

"How's Gatesby?" She cleared her throat.

"Limping, but all right."

"Well, now I know what it feels like to be knocked out." Trish wiggled her fingers and flexed her feet. Everything worked. It hurt to breath deep; in fact, she felt like she'd just been slammed into concrete, not a soft dirt track.

"Where's David?"

"Calling 911."

"Oh, no. Why's he doing that?"

"Trish, you were out cold. What did you expect him to do?"

Trish raised her head.

"I don't think you should move. You know they say accident victims shouldn't be moved."

"Brad, for crying out loud, I'm no victim. I just fell off a horse." She leaned on one elbow. *Ow, that hurt. Not a good idea.* "Here, help me up."

"No, just lie there."

"I have a lump of dirt poking me in the back, the ground is cold, and all my limbs move. Slowly, but they work." She unbuckled her helmet. "Just help me sit up."

Brad slid one arm under her shoulders and cushioned her back as she leaned against him. She pulled her helmet off.

"Good thing I ride with that, huh?" She tossed it aside.

She blinked at the flashes of light in her peripheral vision. Nope, shaking her head was not a good idea, either. She could feel strength returning as she drew in deeper breaths.

"Mostly, I think I had my breath knocked out."

"Trish, it was more than that. You were *out*."

"Well, go tell David . . ."

"Here he comes. You tell him."

"How is she?" David slid to a stop beside them. "They'll be here in a couple of minutes."

"David," Trish groaned. "Call them back. I'm only bruised, not broken. I don't want—" The wail of a siren broke her sentence. "Oh, no. What's Mom going to say now?"

CHAPTER 11

"But Mom, I haven't broken anything."

"What do you call anything? Possible concussion, badly shaken up. Who knows what internal damage. You can hardly move." She spun to nail David with her glare. "What's the matter with you, David? Why didn't you call me?"

"I did."

"After the medics left."

"But Mom, what could you have done? All I could think of was getting medical help when Trish didn't come to." David twisted his class ring on his finger. "You were too far away to do anything. And after they checked her over, they carried her up to the house."

Marge rammed her hands in her pockets and went to stare out the window. "And the paramedics said they didn't think X rays were necessary?"

"That's right."

Trish needed comfort, not this. She could feel the tears damming up behind her eyes again. As she fought them down, the pressure seemed to fill her whole head. She shut her eyes against the pain. A tear squeezed out under a closed lid and trickled down her cheek.

Her mother turned in time to see it. "Oh, Trish, I'm sorry." She dropped down on the side of the bed and wiped her daughter's face with a tissue. "But you scared me half to death." She gathered Tricia into her arms. "I've always been so terrified something like this would happen. Or worse."

Trish clamped both aching arms around her mother's waist and let the tears come. She cried until the pounding drum in her head forced her to lie down again.

Marge handed Trish a handful of tissues and wiped her own eyes with another. "Are you sure nothing is broken?"

"I'm, sure, Mom. But I hurt all over. David says I landed flat out."

"David, go call your father. I'm sure he's worried sick by now." She turned back to Trish. "Would you rather sleep for a while or would you like a hot bath first? That would help the aching."

Trish tried to think but her brain felt fuzzy and she couldn't keep her eyes open. "Later," she mumbled. She wanted to ask how the colt was but her mouth refused to cooperate.

She slept soundly for five hours, her mother checking her daughter's eyes several times for possible signs of a concussion. Those times were only a vague memory. It was thirst that woke her. Trish chewed the grit between her teeth for a moment, opened her eyes very carefully and sighed with relief. The thumping behind her eyes was only a vague impression now.

"Ouch! Ow-w-w!" Every muscle screamed in protest when she tried to sit up.

"Need some help?" her mother asked at the door to her room.

Trish nodded, very carefully.

"I'll get some epsom salts in a hot bath started."

"I'm so thirsty."

"Here, let me help you sit up, then I'll get you a drink. We'll do this in stages." After easing Trish into a sitting position, her feet on the floor, Marge said, "Now wait till I come back before you attempt anything else."

Trish nodded. No danger of that. At least the room had stopped tilting. She flexed her fingers and toes.

The bathroom might as well have been on the moon, it seemed so far away.

———

An hour later, after a long hot soak in the tub, the track dirt washed out of her hair, Trish hobbled back to bed under her own steam. She was out the instant her head hit the pillow.

The bed and bathroom were Tricia's domain until she woke late Sunday afternoon. She stretched, gently checking out each limb. Her arms were still sore, her back and legs ached, but her head was clear. Her stomach—starved. She drank the water left on her nightstand, and slowly rolled over, pushing herself up and easing her feet to the floor. Every back and hip muscle screamed in protest as she stood up. She hesitated, then tottered toward the kitchen, in favor of her hunger pangs.

The note on the counter told her David was at the stables and her mother at the hospital. A plate of food was fixed for her in the fridge.

By the time Trish had eaten and taken a hot shower, she felt fairly close to being human again. Getting up and down from a chair was painful, but not agony. She eased herself down in one and dialed the hospital.

"Dad?" She hesitated at the rough voice that answered the phone.

"Tee, how are you?" Rough voice or not, no one but her father said her name just that way.

"I'll live. I think we ought to sue the truck that ran over me though."

"Thank God you fell so clean. Nothing broken."

"Yeah, I'm lucky."

"Not luck, Trish. You have good guardian angels."

"Yeah, well, it's a shame I didn't land on one of them, it would have been softer than the ground."

"How's Gatesby?"

"I don't know. I just woke up and David's down at the stable."

"Your mom left a few minutes ago. I'm so thankful you're all right."

"How are you doing?" Trish scrunched around on the chair, trying to find a comfortable spot. "You sound awful, but stronger."

"I am. If I do all right through the next three treatments, they're saying I can come home Wednesday."

"Good." Trish nodded. "I miss you." Where were the words to tell him how much she missed him, how much she needed him? The phone was such a poor substitute for the real thing.

"Maybe you'll feel up to coming in tomorrow. I want to make sure none of you are keeping anything from me, like a cast on your arm or leg."

"Dad, we wouldn't do that." Trish grinned at the thought. "The only thing good about a cast would be that you could sign it for me."

"I miss you, Tee." Her father cleared his throat. "Will you come?"

Trish felt the weight of the universe on her shoulders. Her chin sank to her chest. *Go see him*, her little voice nagged. *What's the matter anyway. Scared? What's hard about going to a hospital?*

"Dad, I can't." The words tore at her heart. "I . . . ah . . . I . . ." She fell silent.

"It's okay, Trish, I understand." His voice came softly over the wire. "I'll see you Wednesday, and remember, I love you."

She sniffed and swallowed the tears, almost choking on the boulder at the back of her throat. "Bye." She put the receiver down and her head on her arms. *Why can't I go see him in the hospital? I'm glad he understands, because I sure don't.*

The phone rang again just as she ordered her muscles to stand her up. "Runnin' On Farm."

"Trish, are you all right?" Rhonda's tone carried a note of panic.

"Well, I will be. Right now even this chair needs a pillow. I landed flat-out on my back. At least I've learned first-hand how to fall right. How'd you find out so fast?"

"Brad was just here."

"Hey, how'd the show go?" Trish searched for a more comfortable position.

"Well, I placed in the top ten in the open jumping class."

"How far up?"

"Number ten." Rhonda laughed. "But at least I placed. And one of the other breeders talked to me about riding for him sometime."

"They should. You're one of the best." Trish chewed on her lip. "Sure wish I coulda been there."

"I know. But there'll be other events. How's your dad?"

"May be coming home Wednesday. He sounds awful."

Trish squirmed again. "Hey, my rear's killing me. I'll see you tomorrow. Okay?"

"Bye." The receivers clicked simultaneously.

Trish limped only as far as the kitchen door when the phone rang again. She hesitated only a moment before picking it up. "Runnin' On Farm."

"Hi, Trish," a deep voice said in her ear. "This is Pastor Ron. Just wanted to say we missed you this evening and make sure you're all right."

"I've been better." Trish glanced at the chair and eased her elbows onto the counter instead. "Uh-oh. I just found another bruise."

"Bad, huh?"

"Well, at least nothing's broken. And most of my bruises won't show. I'll probably walk funny for a day or two."

"Trish, we're all praying for your father. The kids met tonight up by the altar for a special prayer session for your dad and for you too."

Trish tried to swallow around her resident lump. "Thanks."

"I'm here when you need me. Remember that."

"Okay."

"I'll see you soon. Tell everyone hello for me. And all of us."

"I will. Thanks." Trish wiped away a renegade tear as she put the phone down.

———

Trish was back at the barns on Monday morning, and although she was moving slowly, she was moving. "Well, Gatesby, old man," she said as she stopped at his stall, "hear you're in about the same shape I'm in. How about a nice walk this afternoon?" She stroked his neck, keeping a firm hand on his nose. She didn't feel like having another bruise on her shoulder.

"He's not limping anymore." David joined her. "I've been bathing his shoulder in liniment. We should have used it on you."

"Should have." She retrieved her goggles and helmet from the tack room. With her jacket sleeve, she rubbed the dust from the helmet. *Good thing I was wearing this thing*, she thought as she secured the chin strap. She snapped her goggles onto her helmet as she approached Spitfire. *I'm sure glad Dad taught us to use every safety precaution. And how to fall. What if I'd tensed up?*

"Your seat feel up to sitting up there?" David asked as she gingerly settled herself into the saddle.

"Not really, but then the thought of a desk at school isn't too hot an idea either." She leaned forward to rub her horse's neck. "And do you think I can get out of either?"

David shook his head. "Just be careful, okay? Work him long and slow and I'll take care of the others." He led her toward the track. "And you *have* to be on time today. I'll signal you at quarter to seven."

"Yes, *mother*." Trish turned Spitfire clockwise on the track and grimaced when he switched from a walk to a trot. Maybe that liniment wasn't such a bad idea.

By Wednesday Trish felt like she was behind by three days again. She used every spare minute at school and if it hadn't been for chemistry, she would have been all right. However, when Brad turned into the drive, her low spirits leaped into high. The family car was parked in front of the house.

Trish just waved in answer to Brad's "see you in a while" and dashed for the door.

"Dad." She barely recognized the man lying in the recliner. Fear clutched her throat and strangled her stomach. She dropped her books on the sofa and tiptoed over to the sleeping figure.

What have they done to you, she almost said aloud. He looked old and broken, like a toy someone had discarded and then hid under a bright quilt. When she touched his hand, she flinched at the deep purple and black bruises on his raised veins.

His eyes flickered open and a barely familiar smile lifted his sagging cheeks. "Tee." She didn't recognize the voice either. It rasped gray, like his face.

Tricia knelt on the floor beside the arm of the chair and laid her cheek on her father's hand. "I'm glad you're home, Dad." She felt his other hand tenderly smooth her hair back from her face. *God!* her soul raged at the heavens. *What have You done to him? I thought You were making him better.*

"I'm just worn out from the treatment today and the trip home. Tomorrow I'll be better, you'll see," he managed.

Trish nodded. "I better get down and work those beasts." She forced herself to drop a kiss on his head. "See you later."

Trish squared her shoulders and kept her stride steady as she left the room. The same iron control enabled her to change clothes and get out the door. The look she gave her mother could have slashed steel.

"David!" She ignored Caesar trotting by her side. She

ignored the nickered greetings from the horses. "David!" Her shout sent Spitfire drumming a heel against the wall. Trish ignored that, too. She jogged the length of the stables to find David down in the yearling pasture. She paused a moment while he latched the gate in front of the two curious colts. Her shout, "David!" cut off his whistle mid-tune.

"What's wrong?" He strode up the lane, breaking into a trot at the expression on her face.

"David Lee Evanston."

He stopped short.

"What'd I do?"

"You never told me."

David reached out and touched her arm. "You've seen Dad."

Trish nodded, her jaw set like a pit bull about to attack. "Why didn't you and Mom tell me how bad he is?"

"We tried. But you wouldn't go see for yourself, remember? We tried to ease you into it. Why do you think Mom's been with him all the time? Trish, for heaven's sake, he has cancer and the doctors think he's going to die."

"My dad's *not* going to die." Trish spun around. The tears she held back threatened to drown her. She fought the bitter bile rising from her stomach and burning her throat. In fact, burning was what she felt all over. Her brain, her heart, down to her toes. Like a forest fire out of control.

"Tee." David tried to stop her.

"Don't call me that." Trish spun away and sprinted down the driveway, her pumping hands pummeling the horror of it all. *Dad calls me "Tee," and you say he's dying.* The thoughts were like flames licking up trees. *He can't be dying. No! God, You don't love us. You don't even care. You're a liar. I hate you!*

CHAPTER 12

"You're in no condition to ride," David said.

Trish finished saddling Dan'l with the western saddle. She'd run for an hour but the fire still flickered. "I'm just taking him down through the woods." She leaned her forehead against the stirrup leathers. "David, just let me be. I promise I won't be stupid with him."

"Okay." He checked the girth. "I . . . Mom . . . we . . ."

"Later, David." She swung up into the saddle. "I'll talk to you later."

Raged out, cried out, worn out, Trish felt empty, spent, exhausted. She put Dan'l away with barely a pat and forced her boots to carry her to the house.

"Where's Dad?" The quiet house seemed to require a whisper.

"He's in bed." Marge looked at her daughter over the top of her magazine. "I'll heat your dinner while you wash up."

"No thanks." Trish looked around as if in a strange country, searching for a familiar landmark. "I'm not hungry."

"Glass of milk?"

"No. I've got some studying to do. See you in the morning." She closed the door softly after a peek at her father. No, he wasn't better.

106

When she came up from working Spitfire in the morning, her father was at his place at the breakfast table. While the plaid shirt he wore looked like it would fit his bigger brother, the smile he gave Trish was more like the father she knew.

"You look like you lost your best friend." The rasp was there but his voice was stronger.

"You're up."

"You're right. Very observant for such an early hour."

Trish wasn't sure whether to run and hug him or run outside and dance for joy. She opted for the hug.

"We're going to be all right," he whispered in her ear, his weak arms using what strength they had to comfort her.

Trish blinked back more tears. She didn't know she had any left. "I gotta hurry."

"So what's new?" He swatted her on the behind as she pulled away.

———

"How's the studying going?" Marge asked that evening after dinner.

"Better." Trish looked up from her chemistry book.

Her mother frowned almost imperceptibly at the piles of clothes in her daughter's room, then sat down on Trish's bed. "Getting better grades in chemistry?"

"Most of the time. It just doesn't make a lot of sense to me."

"It's one of David's favorite classes."

"I guess that's good, since he wants to be a vet." Trish leaned back in her chair. She stretched her arms over her head and yawned.

"How's your back?" Marge cradled her coffee cup in

her hands. "You aren't limping anymore."

"No, the biggest bruise on my hip is more green than purple now. I'm sure glad—"

"That you weren't hurt worse?"

Trish nodded, dreading the turn the conversation was taking. "Don't worry so much, Mom," she pleaded. "It doesn't do any of us any good."

"That's easy for you to say." Her mother sighed deeply. "But no matter how hard I try not to worry, it just doesn't work for me. I close my eyes and I see you flying through the air or landing under some horse's hooves. Trish, accidents *do* happen. You can't deny it." She rose and patted her daughter's shoulder. "And you're the only daughter I've got. I'd just as soon keep you around for a good long time."

"Oh, Mom." Trish turned and wrapped her arms around her mother's waist. She couldn't think of anything else to say.

On Saturday Hal rode in the car down to the stables so he could watch Trish work Gatesby and check on the horses that had recovered from the virus. Neither horse nor girl seemed to remember the falling accident as they broke clean from the gates and breezed the oval track twice, Firefly neck and neck with the bay colt.

David and Trish waved from the last circle of the track as they cooled the horses down.

"I think what we'll have to do is keep them here an extra week," Hal said as the four leaned against the fender of the car in a post workout rehash. Brad, their faithful gateman, had arrived at ten. "We just can't handle the trips back and forth to The Meadows in the morning."

"But will that give them time to get used to the track?"

"It's not the best plan, but in this case, we'll have to take what we can get." Hal started to cough and quickly popped a throat lozenge into his mouth. He wrapped both arms around his chest as if to hold himself together.

"I'd better get back up to the house." The rasp was worse as he fought the urge to cough. He climbed in the passenger side of the pick-up. "Trish, want to drive me up? Let those two strong backs finish the stalls."

Trish hesitated an instant, resentment flaring briefly that he had to leave right when things seemed almost normal. "Sure." She swung into the driver's seat and turned the key.

"Have you made any plans for your birthday?" her father asked as they headed back up to the house.

"No. Not really. I wasn't sure   well, you know . . . who'd be around."

"I know it's been rough on you, Tee. I'd give anything if this weren't so." He sighed. "But it is. Rotten as it seems, we're caught in the reality."

Talk about something else, Trish reasoned in her mind. *Quick, think of something.*

"Uh-h-h, how do you think Gatesby looked?" She stammered in her panic to change the subject.

"Good. You've done a good job with him."

"I still watch him real careful. He nips any chance he gets and spooks at anything . . ." Her voice trailed off as her father opened the passenger door.

"Decide about where you want to go for your birthday dinner. We'll take Brad and Rhonda if you like."

Trish nodded. "Okay." *What I'd like is for you to be healthy again!* she wanted to shout at his stooped back. *That's all I want for my birthday, for Christmas, the Fourth of July. That's all. God, do You hear me? That's all I want.*

"By the way," her father turned back before closing the door. "A Frank Carter called. Said he'd spoken with you about training some horses for him?"

"Yeah, I said you'd call him back but with all that's gone on, I forgot to tell you." Trish leaned her elbows on the steering wheel, dreading her father's answer. "What did you tell him?"

"I told him the truth. That I've been mighty sick and if he can find someone else, he should. Otherwise, call back in a month."

Trish nodded, a tiny smile tickling her cheeks. She nodded again. "Thanks." At least he hadn't said "no way." Her lighter mood fluttered away like a moth on a breeze when she watched her father pause on each step, as if the effort to climb three steps was beyond him. He even leaned on the rail while digging in his pocket for a piece of candy.

Trish forced the truck into gear and drove back down to the stables.

———

Sunday morning the whole family went to church together for the first time in what seemed like months. Trish didn't want to go.

"You're going to make us late," her mother finally snapped. "We'll wait for you in the car."

Trish threw her hairbrush down on the bathroom counter. "I'm coming!" One more honk made her grab her purse and stalk to the car. She paused to see her father sitting on the passenger side. Another change. Too many changes.

She got through the service without really hearing one word. She was amazed at her powers of concentration. In her mind, she'd been at the track with Spitfire the entire time. *So there, God.* So much for worship.

Guilt made her feel like Pastor Ron, their youth pastor, could read her mind as he greeted her after the service.

"See you tonight?" he asked, looking from her to David. "We're playing volleyball at 6:00."

"I wish . . ." Trish looked at David and he was shaking his head too. "I have to spend every spare minute studying so I've time to work the horses."

"We miss you." Ron squeezed her hand. "Take care." He patted David's shoulder. "Both of you."

———

"That mare is going to foal any time," David said at the breakfast table on Wednesday morning. "I'll bring her up to the maternity stall as soon as I take Trish to school." He glanced at his watch. "You're early, kid. What'd you do, turn over a new leaf for your sixteenth birthday?"

"Yup." Trish didn't admit that the reason was because this was the time of day her father looked the best. After his radiation treatments in the morning, he looked bad again, and he was usually asleep when she came home from school. He said his throat was so sore, he had difficulty eating.

"Did you invite Brad and Rhonda for dinner tonight?" her mother asked.

Trish nodded, her mouth full of toast.

"Where do you want to go? I'll make reservations."

"I thought we could go to The Fish House. Their clam chowder is good." Trish had thought about the Mexican restaurant, but it was noisy and the food too spicy for her dad. He wouldn't be able to eat pizza or Chinese food either. "How does that sound?"

"Sounds to me like we better hustle." David jingled his car keys. "You want to drive?"

As Trish eased the car out onto the road, she thought about her dad helping her drive lately and the fact that she hadn't had time to practice more. *I should be taking my driver's test next week!*

Her friends sang "Happy Birthday" to her in the lunchroom. If looks could kill, Rhonda would have been diced meat. She ignored Trish's red face as Doug Ramstead and a couple of other football players came over to claim a kiss.

"I'll get you," Trish hissed, her cheeks hot. Sweet sixteen—how dumb can you get. But inside she felt warm, glad that her friends cared. They'd even brought her a cupcake with a candle and several small presents wrapped and tied with crimson ribbons.

"You guys are awesome." She ignored the tears brimming in her eyes. "Thanks."

"How long till you race?" Doug asked.

"Seventeen days." Trish swallowed at the thought. "We run two weeks from Saturday."

"We'll be there." Everyone nodded.

"Wish we could bet on it," one of the football players said. "Just think, 'Trish to win.' " Someone else took up the chant. "Trish to win. Trish to win. Trish to win." The words swelled around the room. Hands clapped. Feet stamped. Whistlers gave it all they had. The walls reverberated with the din.

Brad and Doug hoisted Trish up on the table so she could be seen by all.

Cheeks flaming, Trish waited for the cheers to die. "Thanks, guys." Her voice rang true in spite of that familiar boulder. She grinned at another whistler. "You are totally awesome. Thanks." She climbed down amid more cheers and whistles. She saw the teachers lined up against the wall. They hadn't even tried to quiet the room down.

"Even the teachers were clapping." She shook her head in amazement as she and Rhonda joined the line at the tray window.

"I know," Rhonda dumped her milk carton in the trash. "We all want you to win. No one from Prairie has ever won a horserace before."

The rest of the day raced by. "See you at seven," Trish tossed over her shoulder as she got out of the car.

"What are you wearing?" Rhonda leaned forward on the seat.

"Denim skirt, I guess. And that rust Shaker sweater."

"Okay. I'll wear a skirt too."

"And I'll wear . . ."

"Shut up, Brad." The two girls chorused and slapped their palms together in a high five.

Trish whistled for Caesar as she ran up the walk. What a birthday.

That night at the restaurant, she looked around at her family, light from the flickering hurricane lamps reflecting off their faces. She could even imagine her father the same as before in the dim light. Until he coughed.

The six of them had been a family for all the years the kids were growing up. Brad and David, she and Rhonda—the four Musketeers.

Trish smelled the carnations in front of her. Both spicy and sweet—just like she felt at the moment.

When the waitress brought a birthday cake with sixteen candles, she wasn't surprised. Everyone sang "Happy Birthday" again and she blew hard, her wish the same as her prayers. *Make my dad well.*

"Oh my!" Her eyes widened as she opened the first of several boxes stacked in front of her. "Racing silks." She lifted the crimson and gold long-sleeved shirt from the tissue paper and held it up. Light glinted off the shiny fabric. She held the shirt to her face, feeling the coolness. "Thanks," she breathed as she laid it back in the box on top of the white pants. She grinned at her father and mother. "They're beautiful."

"Even the right color," Rhonda said. "Open mine and Brad's next."

"A new helmet! Thanks, guys." She smiled and put the hard hat back in its box.

"What do think mine is?" David pointed at the long, slim package left in front of her.

"You sure didn't try to disguise it." Trish lifted a new whip out of the box. "Thanks, David."

She looked around the table. "Now I'm all set. Think how great this stuff will look in the winner's circle! Thank you, everybody."

"Tee, I have something more for you," her father said when they got home. He went into his bedroom and brought out a flat package. Trish looked at him with a question in her eyes. "Go ahead. Open it."

It was a beautiful book with a Thoroughbred's head

on the cover. Inside the pages were blank. Trish had a puzzled expression.

"In all his visits with me at the hospital, Pastor Mort encouraged me to start a journal. Writing things down has helped me in the last few weeks and I thought it might do the same for you."

She flipped through the pages. The fly leaf read, "To my daughter, Trish, with all my love. Dad."

"I wanted to say so much more—"

"The mare's down and in hard labor." David poked his head in the door. "Should be any time now."

Father and daughter stared at each other a few seconds. Matching smiles creased their faces. Trish grabbed both their down vests and they headed out the door together.

"You want to change first?" Hal shrugged into his vest.

"Naw. Let's get down there. Give me the keys and I'll drive." She paused. "Or would you rather walk?"

"I'd much rather walk." Her father dug in his pocket. "But we'd better drive. Here are the keys."

Hal leaned his head back on the seat even on the short stretch to the stables.

A glance at his face in the light from the dash made Trish aware how exhausted he was. Deep lines from nose to chin creased his face. Without a smile to hold the facial muscles up, his skin sagged. While he didn't wheeze, his breathing was shallow and quick. Any exertion made him stop to catch his breath again.

That ever-present snake of fear slithered back to her mind and hissed, *He's dying and there's nothing you can do about it.*

"Dad . . ."

"Um-m-m"

"Do you think you better go back to the house?" She tossed the keys in her palm. "This could be a long wait."

He opened his eyes and reached for the door handle. "Don't worry. Let's go see that mare."

Don't worry. Such an easy thing to say, Trish thought as their footsteps sounded loud in the quiet barn. *And such a difficult thing to do.*

Together they leaned over the stall door. David sat in the deep straw, stroking the mare's head.

"Good thing she recovered so quickly from that virus. She had time to get her strength back," Hal murmured.

"Will that affect the foal?" Trish asked.

"No, it was far enough along to be safe."

As they watched, her body shuddered with the force of the contraction. Two tiny hooves emerged, then withdrew.

"I brought you a stool," David nodded toward the corner. "Trish, come take my place so I can pull if I need to."

"She's progressing well," Hal said softly as another contraction forced the hooves out again. The three of them took their places, ready for an emergency, but relaxed, caught now in a rhythm as old as life.

The mare groaned at the next spasm and a nose joined the hooves. Three more contractions and the foal slid out onto the straw, securely wrapped in its protective sack.

David took a cloth from his back pocket and cleaned the foal's nostrils of mucus. The foal snorted and shook its head.

"It's a filly." He picked up some straw and began scrubbing the foal clean.

"Good girl," Trish praised the mare who lay still through the contraction bringing forth the afterbirth. Then the horse surged to her feet, gave a mighty shake and began nuzzling her offspring. Trish got up slowly, and carefully walked around the two to sink in the straw again at her father's knee.

"What'll we name her?" Trish asked. David left off his scrubbing as the mare took over, cleaning the foal with her tongue. Instead, he tied off the umbilical cord and clipped it with scissors that had been waiting in the pail of disinfectant.

"You name her. She's yours," Hal said.

"Mine?"

"Well, she was born on your birthday. I'd say that old mare gave you a pretty special present."

"Oh, Dad . . ." Trish couldn't get any more words past her resident throat lump.

"I know what to call her." David draped his arms around his knees as he joined them in the corner. "Miss Tee. You know, capital M-i-s-s capital T-e-e."

"Perfect. Trish, meet your namesake." Hal hugged Trish and kept his hand on her shoulder.

Trish watched each movement the foal made. The three of them laughed as Miss Tee propped each toothpick leg and tried to stand. Within an hour she was on her feet, wobbling to her mother's udder and enjoying her first meal. Her tiny brush of a tail flicked back and forth.

The three left the box stall. While David went to get a bucket of warm water for the mare, Trish and Hal leaned on the door to watch the nursing foal.

"With her bloodlines, you should have a real winner there." Hal rested his chin on his hands. "I can see your entry in the programs. Owner, jockey, Tricia Evanston."

"Our entry. We'll have so many by then, Runnin' On Farm'll be famous from Seattle to San Diego. Breeders from all over will be bringing their stock to be trained by Hal Evanston."

Hal remained silent.

Trish trailed off. They had built this dream together, talked it into reality. Spitfire was their great hope this year but next . . .

"Funny how," Hal's voice was a low murmur, like he was talking to himself. ". . . how God brings new life in as old life fades away."

"God didn't do it." Trish snapped. "The mare did." *And quit talking about life fading away,* she wanted to shout at him.

"I'll drive you up." Her flat tone cut each word clean.

CHAPTER 13

Trish didn't talk to her father for two days.

The morning after her birthday he wasn't at the table.

"Your dad had a bad night," Trish's mother explained. "He's finally sleeping."

When Trish pleaded homework in the evening, she wasn't lying. She'd gotten a D on that day's chemistry quiz. And mid-terms were coming up.

She spent every spare minute with the foal. Miss Tee accepted Trish as part of her family and already loved being rubbed behind her ears.

That afternoon Trish brought a soft brush into the box stall. With Miss Tee nearly in her back pocket, she began grooming the mare.

"She's a beauty," Rhonda whispered as she leaned against the stall half-door.

The foal scampered to the far side of her mother at the sound of a new voice. "Isn't she." Trish continued brushing with long, sure strokes. The mare flicked her ears, shifted to relax the other hind leg and went back to drowsing contentedly.

"Do you think she'd let me help you?"

"We can try. There's another brush in the tack room. I'd like to take her out today."

The mare turned to face the newcomer as Rhonda opened the stall door and slipped inside. Rhonda stood perfectly still but carried on a sing-song conversation while the horse sniffed her proffered hand, the brush, up her arm and finally blew in her face.

"You smell other horses," Rhonda said. "And me—I'm no different, just haven't ridden you for a long time." When the mare relaxed again, Rhonda rubbed behind the horse's ears and stroked the brush down her neck.

The little filly peeked out from behind her mother's haunches. She twitched her pricked ears to free them from the veil of her mother's long, black tail draped over her face.

Trish chuckled. "What a sweety."

The two girls chatted quietly, the mare dozed, and the filly became a little bolder toward the strange person who had entered her world.

"You look better now," Rhonda said as they dropped their brushes in a bucket.

"How'd I look before?" Trish asked.

"Bad. What's happened?"

"Well," Trish chewed on the inside of her lower lip, "it seems every time things start to get better, my dad talks about dying or . . ." The tears that seemed to stay right behind her eyelids gathered again. "Or he . . . umm—he's too sick to come to the barn." Straw rustled as the mare moved to the water bucket. The slurp and gurgle of her drinking seemed loud in the otherwise silent barn.

"Rhonda, sometimes I don't even want to talk to him. I don't want to see him . . . see how sick he really is. I *hate* all this." Trish rubbed her fist across her eyes. "And I shouldn't be angry at *him*. Not my dad." She leaned into the mare's neck and let the tears flow.

Rhonda patted Trish's shoulder, her own tears running down her cheeks. "It's not fair," she whispered. "You and your dad, you've always been so special to each other. But Trish, you can't give up. You know we've all been praying. God can work miracles. You can't give up."

"I haven't." Trish sniffed the tears away. "At least not all the time. I pray and keep saying God knows what He's doing and I feel better. Then something happens that knocks me right down again. I feel like a yo-yo. Up and down. Up and down." She felt a tiny soft nose brush her hand. Miss Tee stretched her neck to sniff again.

Trish and Rhonda stood still and let the foal come to them. One tentative step at a time, all the while poised to dart back behind the safety of her mother's tail, the filly approached the two girls.

Trish sneezed.

The foal wheeled on spindly legs and disappeared behind the mare.

"She's just perfect." Rhonda wiped the moisture from her face.

"Yup. At least something's perfect in my life right now." Trish grasped the mare's halter. "Come on, old girl. Let's give you some exercise." She snapped a lead shank on the halter, slid the bolt on the stall door and led the mare out of the stall. The filly glued herself to her mother's shoulder, trying to see everything but keeping herself hidden.

Rhonda opened the small paddock gate so Trish could lead the mare and foal through. The mare braced all four legs and shook herself as soon as the lead shank was unsnapped. The filly darted around the far side of her mother, tiny ears pricked and eyes wide.

Trish and Rhonda leaned against the fence, smiling at the colt's antics.

"Well, I better get going with the others. You want to work Firefly?" Trish asked.

"Sure." Rhonda glanced at her watch. "I've got time. I have to work out in the arena tonight. Dad doesn't like me taking the high jumps without anyone there. Besides, it takes too long to set the poles again by myself."

"Don't knock 'em down and you won't have to get off so often," Tricia teased.

"Thanks for the advice." Rhonda punched her friend on the shoulder. "At least they haven't had to call the paramedics for me."

––––––––

"Don't be jealous," Trish stroked first Spitfire and then Dan'l after all the chores were done that evening and she'd led the mare and foal back in to their stall. "I haven't been ignoring you. Miss Tee's just a baby and babies need lots of attention." She dug in her pocket for a piece of carrot for each of them.

Morning workouts with Spitfire were spent in long conditioning gallops with a final breeze around the track. He fought to go all out but Trish kept him to the schedule her father had set. Unless he sweated up because he was hyper, the black colt was in superb condition, rarely lathering by the end of the run.

––––––––

On Friday night, Trish's father knocked on her door. "Trish, I think it's time we had a talk."

Bent over her chemistry book, she answered, "Sorry, Dad, but I've got to finish this assignment."

Opening her door slowly, her father spoke softly, "I know you've been angry with me."

"Dad, it's not you." Trish turned to face him. "It's this whole . . ." She searched for a good word.

"Mess?"

She nodded. "But please, I can't talk tonight."

"Okay," he agreed. "But I've missed you these last couple of days."

Trish chewed her lip. "I'm sorry." The words didn't come easily.

"Well . . . how about we move the Anderson horses to the track tomorrow? Gatesby's race is only a week away. I ordered the supplies in today."

"Hope he loads okay." Trish perked up now that the discussion was on the horses.

"We'll hood him if we have to. Get to bed early tonight." He pressed her shoulder with a comforting hand.

Trish leaned her cheek on the back of his hand, "I'll try."

That night Trish managed to stay awake for more than a short sentence-prayer. She thought about the good things that were happening: Miss Tee, the workouts, her dad at home and all the friends who helped out and cheered them on. "Thank you, Heavenly Father," she said and named each one. "Thanks, too, for loving me. I'm sorry I've been so angry. Please forgive me? I don't know how to deal with all this. And sometimes I'm so scared. Please make my dad all right again. Amen." She punched her pillow into the right shape, then added, "I almost forgot. Please, God, help Spitfire and me to win the race."

———

The morning fog rolled back as Trish trotted Gatesby out on the track for his early workout. He snorted and slashed at fog tendrils with his front feet.

"Feeling your oats, aren't'cha." She laughed as he leaped sideways at something only he sensed. After a couple of laps, he settled down for the long gallop, repeatedly tugging at the bit whenever he thought Trish might not be paying full attention.

Spitfire gave her the same kind of ride. "What's with you guys today?" She smoothed his mane as they trotted the cooling circle. "David feed you dynamite or something?" Spitfire jigged sideways for a furlong before he settled back to an easy trot. Flecks of lather flew back from where he kept working the bit.

By the time she'd finished Firefly and the three-year-old, Trish felt like she'd done 50 push-ups and 100 chin-ups. She rubbed her arms as she shucked her jacket at the kitchen door.

"Hard workout?" her father asked as she slid into her seat at the table.

"Yeah. They're all really feisty today." She rubbed a particularly tender spot on one shoulder. "And that clown Gatesby snuck by my guard. He wasn't just nipping either."

"He got me when I was cleaning his hooves." David joined them. "And it wasn't my shoulder."

The laughter felt like a little piece of heaven to Trish, and the French toast her mother set in front of her tasted as good.

The comforting scene ended too soon with her father's: "Well, let's load 'em up. That way you can work them both real easy on an empty track this afternoon."

"They're all taped and ready." David shoved back his

chair. "You coming with, Dad?"

"Yes. If I get too tired, I can sleep in the truck."

The loading went amazingly well. When Gatesby saw his stable-mate walk right up the ramp and into the double-wide horse trailer, he followed with only a rolling of his eyes. The shallow pan of grain Brad held out might have contributed to the success.

"You want me to stay here and muck out stalls?" Brad asked as they slammed the tailgate shut.

"Of course not. That's why we have a king cab, to take all of us." Hal waved toward the pickup. "You deserve a break with the rest of us."

"Trish, run in and tell your mother we're leaving," her father said as they stopped at the house.

Why me? Trish thought as she stepped from the vehicle. *This'll give her another chance to worry at me.* She slid the glass door open and leaned inside. "We're leaving, Mom. See you later."

Her mother wiped her hands on a towel, and joined her at the door. "Trish, please watch out for your father." The two of them descended the stairs together. "He gets so tired and I—"

"I know." It felt strange to be on the comforting side for once. "I'll try." Trish climbed back into the truck relieved.

"You all be careful," Marge cautioned when she shut the truck door.

"We will," the three chorused as David shifted into low gear and eased the rig down the drive.

A thrill of excitement, pleasure, and suspense rippled up Trish's spine as they entered the bustling stable area of Portland Meadows Racetrack. When they stopped in front of their five designated stalls, she felt like she'd come home. *My second home, that is,* she hastily amended the thought.

Gatesby backed out of the trailer with his ears flat against his head and hooves thundering on the ramp. Trish handed one lead shank to David and kept up her low murmur, soothing the high-strung animal. Between the two of them, they worked him into his stall. They left him cross-tied in the box, but he let them know his displeasure by a tattoo of hooves on the back wall.

"We'll let him settle while we go do the paperwork," Hal joined Trish after they moved the three-year-old in next door. "John Anderson will be here about 2:00 to watch you work out."

"You mean he's finally back in the country?" She kept her voice light in spite of the knot that tightened her stomach. Riding in front of an owner for the first time was as bad as giving a speech in front of a room full of classmates.

"Right. I know he's gone a lot. But an absentee owner makes it easier for the trainer. You haven't had him trying to tell you how to train his horses."

"True." Trish drew in a deep breath. The mixture of horse, shavings, straw with an overlay of hay, and grain dust smelled better than any perfume to her. She stuck her hands in her back pockets. They were here, and her race was only two weeks away. Right about now she and Spitfire would be riding to the post. She studied a circle she'd drawn in the shavings with her booted toe.

"Scared?" her father's gentle question penetrated her reverie.

"No. Yes." She grinned up at the smile she saw on his face. "Can I be both at once?"

Hal nodded understandingly. "Let's go up to the office and then grab some lunch. Come on, you two."

David and Brad finished moving the tack into the spare stall where their feed and hay had been delivered. Lawn chairs joined buckets along the wall and their two wardrobe-style tack boxes took up another. They hung the Runnin' On Farm sign on the door and joined Hal and Trish.

Back at the barn after a satisfying lunch and their passes in their pockets, Trish felt pure relief at the sight of a note taped on their door that read Anderson wouldn't make it today.

"That's fine with me too." Hal smiled at Trish. "I'm going to rest in the truck for a while. Why don't you start with the three-year-old and come get me when you're ready to work Gatesby." He glanced over at the bay. "Looks like he's calmed down some."

Much to Trish's surprise, the gallops for both animals went smoothly. Gatesby checked out every strange sight, smell, and sound, but once he'd been around the track a couple of times, he acted like an old hand. Trish breathed a sigh of relief as she kicked free of her stirrups and slid to the ground.

Several trainer friends of Hal's had gathered around the box. While the boys groomed the horses, Trish eased over to stand by her father's shoulder. *You're so tired you can hardly spit*, she thought of her dad. *How are you going to get strong enough to get through a race day even as a spectator?* She glanced down the aisle to where David and Brad worked like two arms of the same man. *Guess it's going to be the three of us.* Her jaw tightened. *But we can do it—can't we?*

CHAPTER 14

All Trish wanted to do was crawl back into bed.

She'd fed and watered all the home stock while David took care of the two at The Meadows. When she cross-tied the mare in the alley to clean out her stall, Miss Tee explored her new domain, her tiny hooves dancing through straw wisps and thudding back to hide behind her mother.

Trish threw new straw in the stall, refilled the water bucket and led the mare back in. Miss Tee started her spooking-at-the-straw game all over again.

"You're so silly." Trish dumped a measure of grain into the feed box. While the mare munched, Miss Tee lipped a bit of hay. Trish tugged a couple of strands of straw out of the filly's brush of sorrel mane. "You look like someone gave you a Mohawk." She smoothed the bitty forelock. "Hard to believe you'll ever be big enough to race." Miss Tee whiskered Trish's hand, her nose softer than velvet to the touch. "I'd better go," Trish latched the stall door as she heard the pick-up return, "or they'll be down to get me."

Her mother glanced pointedly at the clock when Trish slid open the glass door. "You've less than an hour," she said as she placed a plate of pancakes in front of her daughter.

128

"How's Dad?"

"Ready and resting. We don't want to be late to church."

Trish flinched at the implied criticism. She wasn't late *all* the time.

Trish's concentration failed her during the sermon. She was right in the middle of a workout with Spitfire when Pastor Mort's voice broke in on her daydream.

"God loves each of us so much He sent His only Son to die a miserable, degrading death—death on a cross. Even Jesus felt abandoned when He cried, 'My God, my God, why have You forsaken Me?' "

Trish tried to put herself back up on Spitfire's back. She couldn't. *Does everyone have to talk about dying?* she thought. But his next words grabbed her back.

"That's how much He cares for you. For each one of us. Look for His promises when you're trapped in the hard spots of life, when everything seems hopeless. Your Bible contains all the promises God has made to His people for all time."

Some care, Trish's thoughts kept pace. *Some promises.*

But you don't know His promises, her inner voice began a debate. *I know some of them,* Trish countered. *Not enough,* the voice insisted.

"Memorize the verses," Pastor Mort continued. "So the Holy Spirit can bring them to your mind when you need them. It is a certain thing that there will be times in life when you need His help, when you need His Word."

Trish got so caught up in the argument in her head, she missed the rest of the sermon. Still, a feeling of warm comfort seemed to settle around her shoulders and snuggle into her mind. How would she find the promises?

She didn't have time to read *all* the Bible right now.

———————

"Wake me in half an hour," Trish tried to stifle the yawn that threatened after lunch. "I need to study before chores."

"And your room?" her mother asked. "If you'd hang up your clothes when you take them off . . ."

"I know." Trish headed down the hall. "I just don't have a lot of extra time." She surveyed the disaster, promised herself to catch up later, and fell on the bed—asleep before she could even roll over.

She awoke two hours later. Silence surrounded her as if she were the only one in the house. She checked David's room. He was sprawled across the bed like a puppet without strings. She peeked into her parents' room. Both of them lay sound asleep too.

Relief flooded through Trish, making her aware she'd been holding her breath. She breathed deeply, returned to her room, and opened her chemistry book. *Might as well use the bit of afternoon remaining.*

She sat down at her desk before she saw it. A green 3 x 5 card was set against her lamp. In her father's block printing were the words: "Cast all your cares on Him for He cares for you" (1 Peter 5:7). She push-pinned the card to the wall so she could see it whenever she looked up.

———————

Trish's alarm rang at 4:30 Monday morning. She stumbled out to the pickup with her eyes half closed and didn't really wake up until David parked the truck at The Meadows. She rode both horses, left them on the hot walker and was back home at exactly seven.

Her first class after lunch was pure agony. Her ump-teenth yawn felt like it would crack her jaw. She got a drink between classes but the chemistry symbols ran together during study hall.

Her head cleared by the time she had Spitfire out on the track, but the evening at her books was an absolute failure. Her mother tapped her on the shoulder. "Trish, you'd sleep better in bed."

Thursday afternoon she fell sound asleep in history class. Rhonda poked her in the back. Trish jerked awake to find the teacher staring at her.

When it happened again on Friday, the teacher said, "Tricia, would you stay after class a minute, please?"

"Oh, no," Trish groaned.

"Tricia, this isn't like you." The teacher leaned against her desk. "I know you're getting ready for the race, but your first responsibility is here, in class."

Trish nodded, her cheeks feeling like she was stand-ing in front of a bonfire. The teacher sounded just like her mother.

"I'll try harder, I really will," she managed.

"I hope so. Otherwise I believe I'll have to talk with your parents." The teacher signed a tardy slip as the bell rang. "Think about it."

"Yes." Trish picked up the paper and left the room. *Oh sure*, she thought. *Talk to my mom. That's all I need. As if I don't have enough on my mind without this. Who needs history anyhow?*

Rhonda waited for her outside their last class. "How bad?"

"She threatened to call my parents if I don't shape up."

"What are you gonna do? You do look beat." Rhonda

held the door open for her friend.

"I don't know, but if she tells my mother, that'll be the . . ." Trish slung her denim jacket over one shoulder. "Let's get out of here." Together they jogged out to Brad's car. "At least it's Friday."

"Don't ask." Trish said to Brad's questioning look.

Trish opened the back door of the house to the aroma of fresh chocolate chip cookies. Her mother pulled a cookie sheet from the oven just as she entered the kitchen.

"Wow, these are great!" Trish relished every morsel. "Thanks, Mom."

"How was school?"

"Okay." Trish poured herself a glass of milk. "Where's Dad?"

"Down at the stable." She turned to put more scoops of dough onto the sheet. "So, what went on today?"

Trish dug a piece of dough out of the bowl with her finger and stuck it in her mouth.

"You might wash your hands first."

"Um-m-m, that tastes good. Seems forever since I've come home to your baking and cooking."

"I know." Marge sighed. "This hasn't been easy for any of us. And Trish, I *am* grateful for all you've done. Even when I don't seem so."

"Thanks, Mom." Trish felt her smile begin way inside and work its way out.

You should have told her about your teacher, the voice admonished.

Well, I got out of that one pretty good, she thought as she went to change her clothes and head for the barn.

————

"I've hired Genie Stokes to ride Gatesby tomorrow," Hal announced at dinner that night. "I decided to stay with a woman since you're the one who trained him, Tee."

"She'll be good for him." Trish laid her fork down. "She taught me a lot last year when we exercised horses together."

"I know. And she has the same light touch you do." Her father leaned his chin on his steepled hands. "She's going to do morning workouts for us too."

"But—" It was hard for Trish to hide her disappointment.

"You're too tired, Tee," he said, glancing toward his wife. "Your mother and I have decided no more morning workouts at the track during school days."

"But what about when we move Spitfire there? We can't have someone else work him."

"I figured we'd move him after school on Wednesday. We'll make an exception for those next two days. Your mother will take you over to ride him and bring you right back. On the condition that you get to bed early both nights."

Trish was afraid to say any more, grateful for the reprieve the two days before the race. No one else had ever ridden Spitfire.

"What about when we have an entry during the week?" she asked.

"Genie will ride then," Marge's voice was firm, to match her expression.

That's not fair! Trish wanted to scream. *They'd let me out of school. My grades are always good enough.*

Oh really, the inner voice intruded. *Flunking chemistry is good enough to get breaks at school?*

Trish looked from her mother to her father. He took his wife's hand in his. "Sorry, Tee. We really believe this is what's best."

Maybe for you, Trish bit her lip to keep the words inside. *But not for me.* "May I be excused, please?" At her parents' nod, she pushed back her chair, rose and left the room, her booted heels beating a staccato pout.

Saturday morning Trish worked the two horses at home before she and Brad went to pick up Rhonda and head for The Meadows. David had gone in at the usual 6:00, and Marge and Hal would be coming closer to post time. Breakfast had been pretty quiet as Trish ate quickly, keeping her eyes on her food to avoid her parents' gaze.

"I'll see you about an hour before post time," her father said. "Then we'll watch the race from the box with the Andersons."

Trish nodded.

"I've already talked with Genie. She knows what I want her to do."

"Fine." Trish left the room without a backward glance, even when she heard her father's deep sigh. *He should be at the track with us all of the time. He's never watched from the box before. And how is he going to do all that walking?* Her thoughts chased around her mind, like chipmunks on a log. Trish rode old Dan'l on the parade to the Post that afternoon. Gatesby seemed to respond well to his new rider—he'd only tried to bite her once. While he jigged sideways, his legs crossing in perfect time, his perked ears showed more interest than orneriness.

"Good luck," Trish waved to the rider as she released the lead. All the instructions had already been given. Trish felt a stir of pride as Gatesby walked easily into the starting gate.

He broke clean at the clang of the gates, his jockey keeping him free of the pack as they rounded the first turn. In this race for maiden colts, he was easy to spot, running slightly to the front. By the fourth furlong, it was obviously a race between Gatesby and a sorrel.

"And they're neck and neck," the announcer intoned. "Numbers five and seven. And they're in the backstretch, ladies and gentlemen."

"Go, Gatesby!" Trish shrieked from her position high on Dan'l's back. Rhonda's shouts joined Trish's from her spot by Dan'l's shoulder. David handed her his binoculars. "Five to win. Come on Gatesby." They chanted in chorus. At the last length, the sorrel surged ahead to win by a nose.

"Oh, no," Trish moaned along with a good part of the crowd.

"For Pete's sake, Tee, he placed, didn't he?" David smacked her on the knee. "That's fantastic! See what a good job you did with him?"

"If you'd been on him, he'd have won," Rhonda said when Trish dismounted and they led Dan'l back to his stall. "Genie may be a good rider, but you know Gatesby."

Trish and David were washing the steaming horse down by the time their father and the Andersons arrived at the stables.

"You've done a fine job with him," John Anderson shook Trish's hand.

"Thank you." Trish grinned up at him. "But it was all of us. We're a team, Dad, David and I. Oh, and Brad and Rhonda, too." She tapped Brad's shoulder as he wielded the scraper. "Besides, Gatesby's a good horse."

"Good and mean." Anderson kept a safe distance from Gatesby's head. "He tried taking a hunk out of me when he was just a little thing."

They all laughed, since each of them had been nipped at one time or another.

"How about you up on him the next time he's out?" Anderson tapped his program on Trish's shoulder. "You trained him, you ride him. Even though the silks will be blue and white instead of crimson and gold. Think that'd be a problem for you?"

"No, sir." Trish shook her head. "No problem at all."

"I'll pay you the standard percentage, of course."

Trish fought to wipe the grin from her face. "That'll be great. Thank you."

"Good for you," her father whispered in her ear as he left with the visitors. "See you at home."

Trish caught the look on her mother's face. Both worry and sadness creased her forehead. *Be happy for me, Mom, will you please?* Trish wished she could have said the words out loud.

Trish ignored the uneasiness she felt around her mother, and embraced the thrill of future mounts to herself as she finished helping with the clean-up. She was on her way to being a professional. Her first mount on a paying basis. The only cloud on her horizon was the gray of her father's face. He looked totally exhausted.

Hal couldn't make it to the dinner table that night, so the family carried dinner to him. Propped up on pillows, the pallor of his face matched the pillowcases, but his smile brightened the room. David parked his TV tray in front of the rocking chair in the corner and Marge pulled up the ottoman.

Hal patted the bed beside him. "Here, Tee. You sit here."

Trish propped pillows against the headboard and wriggled herself into a comfortable position, her tray balanced on her knees. The play-by-play rehash of the day, even though in a different setting than the usual, was the perfect end to an almost-perfect day.

That is, until the others left the room and her father said, "Trish, we have to talk."

CHAPTER 15

In a puff the glow left the room.

Trish stalled for time. "Let me go to the bathroom first." She slipped off the bed. "I'll be right back."

She stalled longer, washing her hands, brushing her teeth and combing her hair. When she finally returned to the bedroom, her father was slumped against the pillows—sound asleep.

"Good-night, Dad," Trish whispered as she shut off the light.

The next afternoon when they returned from church, Hal remained in the front passenger seat. "Come on, Tee. Show me how your driving's improved. Don't rush lunch," he said to Marge as she got out of the car.

"When do you plan to take your test?" he asked Trish as she pulled the car out onto the main road.

"I don't know. When do I have the time?" Trish settled back and relaxed. She loved to drive.

"Probably not this week." Hal rubbed his hand across his face. "Why don't you make an appointment for next Thursday?"

"I have to take the written first, before they'll even schedule my driving test."

"Okay, then plan for the written that day. Are you studied up for it?"

"I think I have the book memorized." Trish flashed a grin at her dad. "Rhonda and I quiz each other."

"Good. Let's stop and get a milk shake at the Dairy Queen and go on out to Lewisville Park."

Trish nodded. She loved the drive to Battle Ground. On a day like today, decapitated Mount St. Helens stood sentinel against the clear blue sky. Vine maple ran rampant up the banks along the road, already flashing vermillion and burgundy.

"Two chocolate, then?" she asked as she stopped the car.

"Yeah. Make it malts."

They pulled into a secluded parking area, easy to find since few picnickers were out this late in the year. For a few minutes the only break in the silence was the slurp of milk shake through their straws.

"How much has your mother told you about my condition?" her father finally asked.

"Not a lot." Trish stirred her shake with the straw.

"Well, the good news is the radiation is shrinking the tumors."

"How much?"

"I couldn't see the difference, but the doctor assured me he saw progress. I keep picturing my lungs healthy, and claiming God's love and healing."

"But David . . . the doctor said . . . but, what if you die? How would *that* show God's love?" Trish stammered over the words.

"I don't know."

"What do you mean you don't know? Aren't you mad? Don't you want to live?"

"Of course. And yes, I have been angry. Angry that this could happen to me. Furious that I kept on smoking even when I knew it was wrong and bad for my health." His sigh came from the pain deep within. "I blamed myself, blamed God, blamed the doctors for not making me well right away."

"But you've always said God can do anything."

"He can."

"And that He loves us."

"He does."

"But what if you die?" Trish gripped the steering wheel like she'd tear it off the column. "How does that show God's love?"

Her father rubbed her shoulder with the hand he'd draped over the back of the seat. "There are no easy answers, Tee. If I die, I get to go home to heaven. I'm with Him then. If I live, I get to stay home with you. Then He's with me. Either way, I'm—we're in His care."

"But I need you here." The cry tore from her heart.

"I know." His voice softened. "I know. And that's my choice too." He gathered her close.

Trish could hear the wheezing as she leaned her head on his chest. *God*, she smothered the thought deep inside her. *If You let my dad die, I swear I'll hate You forever.*

"But, you see, it's not God's fault." Her father had been reading her mind again.

"Then whose fault is it?"

"Sickness isn't anyone's fault. It just exists as long as we're on this earth."

"But . . ." Trish couldn't put her thoughts into words. "I hate cancer."

"So do I."

Trish stared at the container in her hands. "I told God that I hate Him," she whispered.

"I'm sure He understands. He knows our feelings better than we do."

"But—"

"He forgives you, Tee. And He'll never let you go. No matter how much hate and anger you have, He'll take care of it—and you."

"Thanks, Dad." The silence echoed in Trish's thoughts. She looked through the windshield, her gaze focused somewhere beyond the drooping Cedar trees. "You always said God answers prayer."

"He does."

"I've been praying for you to get better."

"So have I. And a lot of other people. You heard Pastor Mort in church this morning."

Trish didn't answer. She'd been careful not to hear much of the service.

"Tee, whichever way it goes, remember that I love you. You'll never know how thankful I've been for the times we've spent together. No man could be prouder of his daughter than I am of you."

Trish let the tears flow. Great sobs shook her entire body as she clung to the father she adored. Tears fell from his eyes too, but he managed to keep from coughing.

When the emotional storm passed, they dried their eyes and attempted to smile. Trish sat up straight and dropped her head on her hands against the steering wheel.

"I still have a hard time seeing that God loves us through all this." Trish turned the key to start the engine.

Her father stayed her hand. "Tee, I've lived my whole life knowing that I am His and He is mine. Why would that change now? I need Him more than ever."

"And I need you."

"I know." He let her turn the key. "But remember that death isn't the end of life."

Trish drove home carefully, her mind a whirlwind of her father's comments.

———

On Monday Trish got to sleep in, and woke to find another card on her desk. This one said: "Fear not, for I am with you. I am your God—let nothing terrify you. I will make you strong and help you. I will protect you and save you" (Isaiah 41:10). She tacked it up above the other one. *How,* she wondered. *How will He do all that?*

David spent Monday and Tuesday evenings coaching her on her chemistry, and his explanations made sense.

"You really like this stuff, don't you?" Trish stared at David as if he were some strange creature from outer space.

"Sure." David scrunched the pillows up behind him against the headboard. "Math and chemistry are orderly—the equations remain the same, if you do them right."

"Yeah, right."

"And yet there are all kinds of realms to explore, like medicine for instance."

"Well since I have no desire to work in medicine or math . . ."

"Besides that, it's good discipline for your mind. You work out to develop your muscles, right?"

"Of course."

"Well, consider this information as a workout for your mind."

"Whether I like it or not, right?" Trish flipped the

pages of her chemistry book back and forth. "Do you think Dad's getting weaker?"

David didn't answer her.

Trish raised her head in time to see and hear her brother draw a ragged breath that seemed to catch on something in his throat.

"Well?" Trish hated the silence filling the room. She knew if David disagreed, he'd have said so immediately.

"Tee," David swung his feet to the floor, but slumped rather than standing up. "That's part of the disease. Dad said the treatments were about as bad as the cancer. They both make him weak."

"I feel like crying all the time. I hate it." Trish slammed her book shut. "I just hate it!"

"I know."

"You, too?"

David nodded.

"But you don't . . . I mean . . . well," Trish met her brother's gaze. The pain she saw mirrored her own. But being of a different nature, he suffered in silence.

On Wednesday, Trish earned a B on the quiz. Things were indeed looking up—in that department of her life, at least.

Snatches of the conversation with her father intruded on her thoughts at odd moments. Like when she was in the shower, or working Spitfire. Or now, when she was supposed to be studying in study hall. *God, he has such faith in You. And he's so sick.*

Last night her father had slept through the workout he'd planned to clock, and right on through the evening. Today he'd gone for a transfusion. And they were sup-

144

posed to transport Spitfire and Firefly to the track when Trish got home.

"It's amazing what new blood and extra rest can do," her father closed his Bible and brought his recliner upright as Trish came through the door.

"You look lots better."

"Feel lots better." He dug in his pocket for one of the perpetual throat lozenges. He didn't wait anymore for the cough to come, but sucked on hard candy or cough drops almost continuously.

"I'll hurry and change."

"Good. David's waiting for us to help load."

Spitfire had to show off a bit as Trish and David led him toward the trailer. He tossed his head and reared with both front feet only inches from the ground.

Trish jerked his lead rope. "Get down here, silly." She gripped the shank right under his halter. "Who're you trying to impress?"

The colt shook his head, his mane flying in every direction. He laid his ears back at the drumming of his hooves on the gate but walked in like an old hand.

Firefly didn't like the idea a bit. As soon as her front feet thudded on the ramp, she backed off with a whinny of protest. Trish led her up to the ramp again and waited for the filly to sniff the ramp. David shook a pan of grain right in front of her nose.

Acting as if she'd never hesitated, Firefly thumped her way into the trailer. Trish breathed a sigh of relief.

"You sure never know what to expect, do you?" Hal shook his head. "You two did a good job with her, with both of them."

"We had a good trainer." Trish shot home the bolt on the tailgate.

After they unloaded the two horses at The Meadows, Trish saddled Spitfire and took him out on the empty track. The colt paid attention to her voice and hands, but his twitching ears recorded all the new sights and sounds. He shied at a blowing program and snorted at the snapping flags on the infield. Trish kept him at a slow jog.

"This way there'll be no surprises for you, old buddy." She stroked his neck with one gloved hand. "You just check it all out now, 'cause Saturday we're going to be going so fast you won't have time to look."

That night Trish woke to the sound of her father's coughing. She got up and tiptoed down the hall. Her parents were both dressed.

"I'm taking your dad in to Emergency. We can't get the coughing to stop," her mother said as she helped her dad into his jacket. "I'll call you as soon as we know anything."

"You want me to drive?" David stumbled from his room.

"No. You stay with Trish." Marge tucked her purse under her arm.

"Don't worry, you two," Hal rasped between breaths. "I'll be at the track even if it's in a wheelchair."

Trish had a hard time going back to sleep. *God, he looks so awful. Please don't let him die now. Please. Please.*

When her alarm went off, she could smell bacon frying. Trish peeked into her parents' room on her way to the kitchen. Her father was asleep in the bed, a portable metal tank on the chair beside him, and a tube with prongs to his nose.

"What happened?" Trish asked when she entered the kitchen.

"They gave him some medication and oxygen, and tried to keep him there. But, as you see, your father is pretty stubborn." Her mother slipped the platter of bacon into the oven to keep it warm. "So hurry up now. I've made a good breakfast this morning."

Trish felt like the four Musketeers were together again as she and Rhonda prepped Spitfire, and David and Brad worked on Firefly for the afternoon workout. They saddled Spitfire first.

"Loosen him up with a couple jogs around, slow gallop twice, and let him out for four." Hal gave Trish specific instructions. "We'll clock him."

"Forty flat," her father said before Trish could ask. "Do you think he was all out?"

"No." Trish smoothed her mount's sweaty mane. "He does better on the longer distances and with someone else pushing him."

Genie Stokes had joined the group at the rail. "He sure looks good, Trish. Did you know I'll be riding against you Saturday? That'll be a great race."

Trish could feel her insides tighten up. Any mention of Saturday brought the same reaction.

"Hey, don't worry." Genie patted Trish's knee as she guided Spitfire back to the stalls. "You'll do just fine."

"Thanks." Trish dropped to the ground and let David take the colt to his stall and begin cooling him down. "How's Gatesby doing?"

Genie rubbed her shoulder. "You sure you want to know?"

"Up to his old tricks?" Trish laughed. "You gotta watch that Gatesby."

"Can you two come for dinner?" Hal nodded at Brad and Rhonda when they were all ready to leave. "We'll get some take-out pizza."

Trish and Rhonda grinned at each other. Brad nodded.

"Good. Stop and get whatever you want." Her father stuffed some bills in Trish's hand. "Get some soft drinks too."

———

Feels like old times, Trish thought, after most of the three giant pizzas had disappeared. A fire snapped and crackled in the fireplace. Her father rested in his recliner, her mother's rocker creaked familiarly. All four young people lounged against floor pillows, and David fed the empty paper plates and pizza boxes into the fire. It felt so good, Trish was able to ignore the gray lines on her father's face.

"I want to thank all of you for all the extra work you've done around here," Hal said. "We couldn't have made it without you. Brad, Rhonda, you've been like my own kids ever since you were young."

"Yes, I had four chicks to worry about, not just two." Marge joined the laughter. "You've been busy kids."

"Still are," Hal added. "I'm really proud of all of you. And now, I'm going to call it a night." He brought his recliner upright. "See you at the track tomorrow."

"Thanks for the pizza," Rhonda said, finishing her drink. "Come on Brad. Trish needs her sleep."

"Yeah, so she'll look beautiful in the winner's circle tomorrow." Brad tossed his paper cup in a wastebasket.

Trish hugged the warm glow of the evening around her as she snuggled under her bed covers. *Just like old times. Thank you, Heavenly Father. Thank you.* Repeating the words lulled her to sleep. She felt like she'd just dozed off when she felt someone shaking her.

"Trish. Wake up." David shook her again.

"What?" She sat up, blinking at the light from the hallway.

"Dad's bad again. He and Mom are about to head back to the hospital."

Trish leaped from her bed and padded down the hall. She could hear her father fighting to breathe as she reached their room. He sat hunched over on the edge of the bed, the oxygen in place. Trish noticed a blue tinge to his lips. She took his hand, wrapping it in both of hers to warm it.

"I'll—see—you—in—the—morning." He panted between gulps of air. "Or—at—the—track." He draped his arm across her shoulders as David helped him to his feet. Between the two of them, they helped him to the car and swung his legs in. Trish dashed back into the house for a quilt.

"Here," she said, wrapping the blanket around him and hugging him once more.

David draped his arm around her as they waved at the receding taillights. "Pray for all you're worth," he said.

CHAPTER 16

Her parents' bedroom was empty when Trish checked in the morning.

She'd fallen asleep just as dawn pierced the darkness of night. Now everything looked gray, overcast, fog hugging the hollows. Trish felt gray inside, even though her resident butterflies were already up and about.

"Has Mom called?" she asked as she joined David in the kitchen.

"No." He checked his watch. "Can you be ready in half an hour?"

Trish mixed a glass of instant breakfast and forced it down. The thought of chewing even a piece of toast made her gag. After her shower, she packed her silks—the crimson and gold high-necked shirt, the white stretch pants. She snapped the silky cover in place on her helmet and tucked it in. She'd carry her boots and whip.

By the time they arrived at the back gate she'd chewed two fingernails down to the quick. The guard waved them through.

Trish could see that Brad had been hard at work when they opened the door to their tack room. All the stalls had been mucked out, and all four of the animals were out on the hot walker.

"Thanks." Trish patted her friend on the back as he

forked the last of the clean straw back into one of the stalls. "How'd you get done so fast?"

"Slave labor." Rhonda squeezed past the wheelbarrow and stuck her pitchfork in the heap of straw and manure. "How're you doing, Trish?"

"I don't know." Trish shook her head. "One minute I think I'm going to throw up and the next that I'll faint. I've never had the shakes so bad."

"Better get 'em over with now." Brad leaned on the handle of the pitchfork. "Once you start working with the man," he nodded at the black colt playing with the ring on the walker, "you'll be fine. He's in great form today."

"I keep telling myself this is our day for winning. Dad and I . . ." her voice choked.

"He'll be here, Trish," Brad promised. "He said he would, and you know what an iron will he has."

"Something like yours," Rhonda finished as she gave Trish a hug.

Brad wrapped his arms around both girls. "You and your dad, you're two of a kind, Trish."

Trish leaned into the comfort and warmth of her friends' embrace. As she breathed deeply, she inhaled all the aromas of the track, and Brad's woodsy aftershave. She made herself take even breaths and with each exhalation, the tension drained away, bit by bit.

"Thanks again." She hugged first Brad, then Rhonda, and drew herself up to her full height. "Well, Spitfire. Let's get at it."

When they'd finished grooming Spitfire, the rising sun sparked blue highlights in his black coat. He tossed his head and nickered at the horses passing back and forth in the aisle. When David picked up Spitfire's front hoof to clean it, the colt gave him a nudge that sent him to his knees.

"He's just having fun." Trish giggled at the look of disgust on her brother's face. "He thinks it's time to play."

"Well, you can do your playing out there on the track." David planted his feet more firmly as he raised the next hoof. "Trish, hang on to him."

When they were finished, they draped the sheet over the perfectly groomed horse and cross-tied him in his stall.

"You want to get some lunch?" David asked.

Trish stared at him as if he'd lost his marbles.

"Just thought I'd ask." He sat down in one of the chairs in the tack room. "Brad, you want to saddle Dan'l for the post ride?"

"Sure thing."

"And lead them in the parade to the post." David glanced at Trish. "That okay with you?"

"Fine." Trish swallowed. The butterflies were back.

"Here." Rhonda handed Trish a neon-pink plastic water bottle. "It's lemonade. I'm always thirsty just before an event and cola makes me more hyper."

"Thanks," Trish said before taking a deep swallow through the attached straw. "You're right. This was just what I needed."

"How are the butterflies?" Rhonda rolled her eyes to make Trish laugh.

"Fluttering."

"Noon." David announced after glancing at his watch. "You better get over to the dressing room. "I'll call the hospital before I bring Spitfire over to the saddling paddock. We'll see you there."

"Okay." Trish gathered up her carry-all, whip and boots. "You'll bring the saddle and pad?"

"And your number. Three was a good draw."

"Dad's favorite number." Trish chewed her lip. The walk across the infield to the stands and the dressing rooms seemed like a mile. Or more.

"You want me to help carry your stuff?" Rhonda asked.

"You ready, Trish?" Genie Stokes stopped at their door.

"Sure am." Trish breathed a sigh that sounded strangely like a swimmer who'd just snagged a lifebuoy. "Thanks anyway, Rhonda. See you guys over there."

"I remember what my first race was like," Genie said as they walked past the stables. "I was absolutely sure I was gonna throw up. And then I was afraid I wouldn't. Did you eat something this morning?"

"Yes." Trish found herself answering in monosyllables.

"Good. I'd grab a bite with you after the race, but I'm riding three different horses today. Pretty good, if I do say so."

Laughter and the pungent odor of liniment hit them as they opened the door to the women's dressing room. Trish hung her things on a hook and joined Genie in an open area where several women were stretching out. She felt her stomach relax as she touched her head on her knee for hamstring stretches. The familiar routine warmed her body and the jokes flying around brought first a smile, then a giggle.

Genie introduced her to the others and helped her begin to form a routine of her own.

When Trish left the room to go pick up her saddle,

she took one last glance in the full-length mirror. No one would know she was a novice from her appearance. She brushed a hand through her dark hair and snapped the helmet in place.

Brad whistled under his breath as he handed her the saddle. "Let's walk before I weigh in." Trish checked her watch. "I have extra time. How's Spitfire?" she asked. "And Dad."

"Spitfire's ready to race and no report on your father. David couldn't get hold of your mom."

"That must mean they're on their way here." Trish nodded.

"You look totally awesome." Brad stepped back to look her up and down. "Wait till the team sees you."

"They're here?"

"Right on the other side of the paddock. Can't you hear them?"

"Trish to win. Trish to win." The chanting grew louder as they walked down the tunnel.

Trish waved as they paused in the entrance to the paddock. The saddling stalls formed a circle like spokes of a wheel. On the other side, spectators could come to watch behind-the-scenes action. Students from Prairie High lined the rails.

"You better go quiet them down," she told Brad. "I have to go weigh now." She waved to her cheering audience one more time. "See you in a bit."

"Good luck." Genie shook Trish's hand after they'd both been weighed in and lead weights inserted in the slots of their saddle pads.

"Same to you." Trish carried her saddle over for David to settle it just behind Spitfire's withers. As he tightened the girth, she stroked Spitfire's muzzle one more time. "This is it, fella." She smoothed his forelock. "So give it all you got."

"You can do it." Rhonda accompanied her assurance with a hug. "You're winners, both of you."

"Thanks." Trish felt like her smile might slide off and get buried in the dirt.

David boosted her atop her mount and held the stirrup while she settled her feet in place. "Now, you remember all Dad's instructions?" He patted her knee.

Trish nodded and took another deep breath before she picked up the reins. She patted Spitfire's neck again as David untied the lead rope and handed it over to Brad. After snapping her goggles in place, she nodded again.

Dan'l stepped smartly into the number three place in line when the bugle called the parade to the post. As they cleared the dim tunnel and came out into the sunlight, Trish blinked and checked the box reserved for Runnin' On Farm. It was still empty. Her father wasn't standing along the fences leading to the track either.

Trish had no more time to search. Spitfire danced sideways in his personal ballet. "Easy, boy." Her continual murmur seemed to entertain him as his ears flicked back and forth at her words. His black hide gleamed, already damp from the excitement.

As they pulled even with Dan'l, Brad grinned at her. "You're gonna do it, buddy." He snugged the lead rope down to keep Spitfire from drawing ahead. "You two look better than anything out here." He unsnapped the lead shank as they turned and slow-galloped back toward the gates. His thumbs-up signal to Trish meant "to win."

God, take care of my dad was Trish's only thought as she snuck one last glance at the empty box. Spitfire strutted into the gate and only blew when the metal clanged shut behind him. Trish felt him settle for the break. She concentrated on the space between his cocked ears, willing both herself and the horse to victory.

The shot and the opening clang of the gates sent the field surging from the gates. Spitfire broke at just the right moment, with a mighty thrust that gave them the rail in three strides. Horses one and two disappeared in the melee.

Trish leaned over the colt's withers, her face buried in his blowing mane. As they rounded the first turn she sensed a horse on their right, coming up strong. "Let's go, fella." She loosed the reins a bit and was rewarded with another lengthening of the colt's stride.

She could hear her father's voice: "Save him for the final stretch, if you can. But he likes to be out in front, so do what feels right."

They rounded the far turn with Spitfire running easily, his ears up and twitching between Trish's running cadence and his observing everything around him. He tugged at the bit but didn't fight when Trish kept her hands firm. Still she felt him settle a bit deeper as his stride lengthened.

Coming down the final stretch, Trish became aware of a horse pulling up on the outside. He was flattened out, the jockey using the whip to bring out the last reserves.

"Go, boy!" Trish shouted to her mount. "Come on."

As they flew across the finish line, Trish wasn't sure who'd won. They'd pounded the last yards nose and nose. She stood in her stirrups to bring Spitfire down to a canter and circled back toward the stands.

"I'm sorry, fella," she tightened the reins as he tugged

on the bit. "I should have let you go when you wanted. Your hearing is better than mine. If we lost, it's my fault, not yours."

"We have a photo finish, ladies and gentlemen," Trish heard the announcer. "That's numbers three and five. A photo finish—we'll have the results for you in just a couple of minutes, so hang on to your tickets."

Trish wiped lather from her cheek and let Spitfire trot around in a circle. The other horses, except for number five had left the track.

"Trish! Trish! Trish!" The chant gained momentum as the cheering crowd quieted. The block of crimson-and-gold-clad teenagers roared from their seats. "Trish! Trish!"

Trish smoothed Spitfire's mane and allowed herself a glance at the stands. The box was still empty. She started to check the fences, but the announcer's voice cut into her concentration.

"And the winner of the first race today for maiden colts is *number three.* Spitfire—bred and owned by Hal Evanston and ridden by Tricia Evanston."

Trish's response to her victory was different than she thought it would be. As she walked Spitfire into the winner's circle, all she could think of was her father. Her eyes scanned the box one last time. It was empty.

And then she saw him. Straight ahead, between Spitfire's twitching ears, her father shuffled forward, braced by David on one side and her mother on the other. Trish's smile was brighter than the flashing of cameras as she slid to the ground.

While the steward settled the horseshoe of red roses over Spitfire's withers, Trish clutched the reins right under her mount's chin with one hand and reached for her father's hand with the other.

"Good job, Babe." He squeezed her hand. "I knew you could do it." Spitfire snorted and rolled his eyes as the flashbulbs flared. He nosed Hal's shoulder, then lipped the hair that fell beneath Trish's helmet. When he tossed his head, a gob of lather landed on Marge's cheek.

"You goof." Trish rubbed the colt's soft nose. "You're a celebrity now, so act cool." She caught her mother's eye as she wiped the lather off her face.

"Good race, Trish," Marge said as she wiped her hand on her husband's sleeve. "Thanks a lot, Spitfire. I needed that."

Trish, David, and Hal looked first at Marge, then at each other. While they tried to appear professional for the final shots, laughter linked them as securely as the arms that locked them each to the other.

The Evanstons had won their race.